Me and My Girl

Book and Lyrics by
L. Arthur Rose & Douglas Furber

Music by
Noel Gay

Book revised by
Stephen Fry

Contributions to revisons by Mike Ockrent

Natalie Kastner

A Samuel French Acting Edition

SAMUELFRENCH.COM
SAMUELFRENCH-LONDON.CO.UK

Copyright © 1954 by L.Arthur Rose and Douglas Furber
Copyright © 1982 by Dr. Ian Rose and Mortimer Lewin Furber
Copyright © 1986, 1990 by Estate Music Co., Ltd.
All Rights Reserved

ME AND MY GIRL is fully protected under the copyright laws of the United States of America, the British Commonwealth, including Canada, and all other countries of the Copyright Union. All rights, including professional and amateur stage productions, recitation, lecturing, public reading, motion picture, radio broadcasting, television and the rights of translation into foreign languages are strictly reserved.
ISBN 978-0-573-68910-9
www.SamuelFrench.com
www.SamuelFrench-London.co.uk

FOR PRODUCTION ENQUIRIES
UNITED STATES AND CANADA
Info@Samuelfrench.com
1-866-598-8449
UNITED KINGDOM AND EUROPE
Plays@SamuelFrench-London.co.uk
020-7255-4302

Each title is subject to availability from Samuel French, depending upon country of performance. Please be aware that *ME AND MY GIRL* may not be licensed by Samuel French in your territory. Professional and amateur producers should contact the nearest Samuel French office or licensing partner to verify availability.

CAUTION: Professional and amateur producers are hereby warned that *ME AND MY GIRL* is subject to a licensing fee. Publication of this play(s) does not imply availability for performance. Both amateurs and professionals considering a production are strongly advised to apply to Samuel French before starting rehearsals, advertising, or booking a theatre. A licensing fee must be paid whether the title(s) is presented for charity or gain and whether or not admission is charged. Professional/Stock licensing fees are quoted upon application to Samuel French.

No one shall make any changes in this title(s) for the purpose of production. No part of this book may be reproduced, stored in a retrieval system, or transmitted in any form, by any means, now known or yet to be invented, including mechanical, electronic, photocopying, recording, videotaping, or otherwise, without the prior written permission of the publisher. No one shall upload this title(s), or part of this title(s), to any social media websites.

For all enquiries regarding motion picture, television, and other media rights, please contact Samuel French.

RENTAL MATERIALS

An orchestration consisting of **Piano/Conductor Score, Reed 1 (Piccolo, Flute, Alto Sax, Clarinet), Reed 2 (Flute, Alto Sax, Clarinet), Reed 3 (Oboe, English Horn), Reed 4 (Tenor Sax, Bass Clarinet, Clarinet, Oboe, Flute), Reed 5 (Baritone Sax, Clarinet, Bassoon), Violin, Cello, Bass (Fender/Acc.), Harp, Horn, Guitar, Trumpets 1, 2, and 3, Trombone, Keyboards 1 and 2, Trombone 2, Percussion, Drums, and 30 vocal/chorus books** will be loaned two months prior to the production ONLY on the receipt of the Licensing Fee quoted for all performances, the rental fee and a refundable deposit. Please contact Samuel French for perusal of the music materials as well as a performance license application.

MUSIC USE NOTE

Licensees are solely responsible for obtaining formal written permission from copyright owners to use copyrighted music in the performance of this play and are strongly cautioned to do so. If no such permission is obtained by the licensee, then the licensee must use only original music that the licensee owns and controls. Licensees are solely responsible and liable for all music clearances and shall indemnify the copyright owners of the play(s) and their licensing agent, Samuel French, against any costs, expenses, losses and liabilities arising from the use of music by licensees. Please contact the appropriate music licensing authority in your territory for the rights to any incidental music.

IMPORTANT BILLING AND CREDIT REQUIREMENTS

If you have obtained performance rights to this title, please refer to your licensing agreement for important billing and credit requirements.

Book Copyright © 1954 by L. Arthur Rose and Douglas Furber; 1982 by Dr. Ian Rose and Mortimer Lewin Furber; 1986, 1990 by Estate Music Co., Ltd.

Lyrics:

"Me and My Girl" and "The Lambeth Walk" Copyright © 1937, 1965 by Cinephonic Music Co., Ltd. and Richard Armitage, Ltd.

"Once You Lose your Heart" and "Song of Hareford" Copyright © 1953 by Noel Gay Music Co., Ltd. and Richard Armitage, Ltd.

"Loves Makes the World Go Round" Copyright © 1938, 1966 by Noel Gay Music Co., Ltd.

"Hold My Hand" Copyright © 1931, 1958 by Chappell Music,Ltd. and Richard Armitage, Ltd.

"The Sun Has Got His Hat On" Copyright © 1932, 1959 By West's, Ltd. and Richard Armitage, Ltd.

"Leaning on a Lamp-Post" Copyright © 1937, 1965 by Cinephonic Music Co., Ltd. and Richard Armitage. Ltd.

"Thinking of No One But Me", "A Weekend at Hareford", "The Family Solicitor", "You Would if You Could", "An English Gentleman", and "Take It on the Chin" Copyright © 1937 by Cinephonic Music Co., Ltd. and Richard Armitage, Ltd.

ME AND MY GIRL opened August 10, 1986 at the Marquis Theatre, New York City, with the following cast:

LADY JAQUELINE CARSTONE	Jane Summerhays
THE HON. GERALD BOLINGBROKE	Nick Ullett
STOCKBROKERS	Cleve Asbury, Randy Hills, Barry McNabb
LORD BATTERSBY	Erick Hutson
LADY BATTERSBY	Justine Johnston
HERBERT PARCHESTER	Timothy Jerome
SIR JASPER TRING	Leo Leyden
MARIA, DUCHESS OF DENE	Jane Connell
SIR JOHN TREMAYNE	George S. Irving
CHARLES HETHERSETT, THE BUTLER	Thomas Toner
FOOTMAN	Larry Hansen
BILL SNIBSON	Robert Lindsay
SALLY SMITH	Maryann Plunkett
PUB PIANSIT	John Spalla
MRS. WORTHINGTON-WORTHINGTON	Gloria Hodes
LADY DISS	Elizabeth Larner
LADY BRIGHTON	Susan Cella
BOB BARKING	Kenneth H. Waller
TELEGRAPH BOY	Bill Brassea
MRS. BROWN	Elizabeth Larner
LAMBETH GIRL	Susan Cella
CONSTABLE	Eric Johnson

The Ensemble: Cleve Asbury, Bill Brassea, Jonathan Brody, Frankie Cassady, Susan Cella, Sheri Cowart, Bob Freschi, Ann-Marie Gerard, Larry Hansen, Ida Henry, Randy Hills, Gloria Hodes, K. Craig Innis, Eric Johnson, Michael Hayward-Jones, Barry McNabb, Donna Monroe, Barbara Moroz, Cindy Oakes, William Ryall, John Spalla, Cynthia Thole, Mike Turner, Kenneth H. Waller. Swings: Corinne Malancon, Tony Parise

Directed by Mike Ockrent; Choreography by Gillian Gregorey

Set design by Martin Johns, Costume design by Ann Curtis, Lighting design by Chris Ellis and Roger Morgan, Musical direction by Stanley Lebowsky, Orchestrations and Dance Arrangements by Chris Walker, Casting by Howard Feuer

General Manager, Ralph Roseman; Production Stage Manager, Steven Zweigbaum; Dance Assistant, Karin Baker; Dance Captain, Tony Parise; Assistant Musical Director, Tom Helm.

SCENES AND MUSICAL NUMBERS

The action takes place in the late nineteen thirties, in and around Hareford Hall, Hampshire, Mayfair, and Lambeth

ACT I

PROLOGUE	MAYFAIR
Scene 1	HAREFORD HALL, HAMPSHIRE
	"A Weekend At Hareford......The Ensemble
	"Thinking of No One But Me"....Lady Jaquie and Gerald
Scene 2	THE KITCHEN
	"An English Gentleman".....Hethersett and Staff
Scene 3	THE DRAWING ROOM
	"You would if You Could"....Lady Jaquie and Bill
	"Hold My Hand"....Bill, Sally and Dancers
Scene 4	THE HAREFORD ARMS
	"Once You Lose Your Heart"
Scene 5	THE TERRACE
	"Preparation Fugue"...The Company
	"The Lambeth Walk"....Bill, Sally and Company

ACT II

Scene 1	THE GARDEN AT HAREFOLD HALL, the next afternoon
	"The Sun Has Got His Hat On"....Gerald, Lady Jaquie and Ensemble
	"Take It On The Chin"....Sally
Scene 3	THE LIBRARY
	"Once You Lose Your Heart" (reprise)...Sally
	"Song of Hareford....Duchess, Bill and Ensemble
	"Loves makes The World go Round"...Bill and Sir John
Scene 4	HAREFORD HALL, weeks later
Scene 5	HAREFORD HALL, shortly after
	"Finale".....The Company

ACT I

[MUSIC CUE #1—OVERTURE]

Scene 1

Mayfair, on the road to Hareford, and Hareford Hall. A summer's evening.
The curtain rises, and we see the GUESTS grouped in and around a large open touring car. A POLICEMAN stands nearby.

(End overture: CREW CUE: 1)
(then: ELEC CUE: 1)

[Music CUE #2: A WEEKEND AT HAREFORD]

LADY #1.
THE SEASON IN LONDON HAS STARTED TO BORE
LADIES #2,3,4.
THERE'S NOTHING TO DO THERE YOU'VE NOT DONE BEFORE
STOCKBROKERS.
THE PEOPLE ARE TIRESOME
LADIES #1-4.
THE PARTIES A CHORE
ALL.
WE JUST COULDN'T STAY THERE FOR ONE MINUTE MORE
GENTLEMEN.
THE WEEKENDS IN LONDON HAVE LOST ALL THEIR FUN
LADIES.
NOW WIMBLEDON'S OVER
GENTLEMEN.
THE TEST MATCH IS DONE
NOW HENLY HAS FINISHED

LADIES.
AND ASCOT HAS RUN
　　ALL.
IT'S TIME FOR THE COUNTRY, IT'S TIME FOR THE SUN

(*A STOCKBROKER GUEST cranks the car to a start, the POLICEMAN is left behind, and the GUESTS are on their way to Hareford.*)　　(ELEC CUE: 2)

　　ALL.
THERE ISN'T ANY DOUBT
ABOUT THE BEST PLACE TO GO
　　GENTLEMEN #1-3.
IT'S HAREFORD HALL IN HAMPSHIRE
WHERE THE SMART PEOPLE GO
　　LADIES # 1&2.
IF THE DUCHESS DOES INVITE YOU
THEN YOU'RE TOP OF THE TREE
　　ALL.
THANK GOODNESS, THANK GOODNESS
SHE DID WRITE TO ME
SHE DID WRITE TO ME
　　GENTLEMEN.
THE ATMOSPHERE WILL LIGHTEN
WHEN WE REACH HAREFORD HALL
　　LADIES.
AND EVERYTHING WILL BRIGHTEN
WHEN WE'RE ALL AT THE BALL　　(ELEC CUE:3)
　　　　　　　　　　　　　　(CREW CUE: 2)

(*The car arrives outside the gates of Hareford Hall. The GUESTS dismount revealing a car composed of a number of pieces of luggage which are quickly disposed of by STAFF and GUESTS.*)

　　ALL.
YOU'LL FIND NO ONE WILL FORCE YOU
TO WAKE UP AT DAWN

THERE'S BREAKFAST IN BED AND
THERE'S LUNCH ON THE LAWN
    LADY #2.
AND IF THERE ARE INCHES
YOU'D LIKE TO WORK OFF
THERE'S SWIMMING
    GENTLEMEN #4.
THERE'S CROQUET
    LADY #1.
THERE'S TENNIS
    GENTLEMEN #1
AND GOLF
    GUESTS, STAFF.
WITHOUT EQUIVOCATION
WE CAN ALL RECOMMEND
THE NOBLE INSTITUTION OF
THE HAREFORD WEEKEND

IT HAS ITS SOCIAL EQUAL
NOWHERE ELSE IN THE LAND
THERE'S NO OTHER HOME
SO STATELY AND GRAND   (CREW CUE: 3)
SO STATELY AND GRAND   (CREW CUE: 4)

(The gates open revealing the exterior of Hareford Hall.)

    GUESTS.
THE ATMOSPHERE HAS HEIGHTENED
NOW WE'RE NEAR HAREHORD HALL
THE YOUNGER GUESTS ARE FRIGHTENED
WE'VE NOT BEEN HERE AT ALL   (ELEC CUE: 4)

(The center doors of the Hall open and LORD and LADY BATTERSBY, SIR JASPER TRING, LADY JACQUELINE, HETHERSETT, and HOUSEKEEPER emerge to greet their GUESTS. GERALD can be seen looking out from an upstairs window.)

FAMILY, GUESTS, STAFF.
BUT YOU'RE WELCOME SO LONG AS
YOU KEEP TO THE RULES
THE DUCHESS HAS NEVER
BEEN PARTIAL TO FOOLS (CREW CUE: 5)
BUT REALLY SO LONG AS (ELEC CUE: 5)
YOU KNOW WHAT IS DONE
YOU'RE HAPPY ENJOYING
YOUR PLACE IN THE SUN

(The house revolves to display the interior of Hareford Hall. There are ancestral portraits on the walls, and a suit of armour to the left of the center entrance. The room is furnished with two long tables set as for a grand buffet, a number of dining chairs, and an occasional table with a vase of flowers and a letter rack.)

ALL.
FOR A WEEKEND AT HAREFORD
IS SIMPLY DIVINE
THE PEOPLE, THE PARTIES,
THE FOOD AND THE WINE
THERE'S LEISURE AND PLEASURE
FOR EVERYONE
YOU'RE HAPPY ENJOYING
YOUR PLACE IN THE SUN
    JAQUIE.
IT DOES SEEM SUCH A PITY THAT
THEY CAN'T FIND THE HEIR
THE FAMILY SOLICITOR
HAS LOOKED EVERYWHERE
    ALL MEN.
IT'S RUMOURED AT THE MOMENT
THAT HE'S TEARING AROUND
    ALL.
THE DUCHESS DEMANDS
THAT THE HEIR SHALL BE FOUND

THE HEIR SHALL BE FOUND (ELEC CUE: 6)
   GERALD. (*On balcony.*)
LISTEN EVERYBODY
FOR THE NEWS WILL SOON BE 'ROUND
THE FAMILY SOLICITOR
HAS RUN THE HEIR TO GROUND
THERE'S NOT A DOUBT ABOUT IT
THERE ISN'T ANY SNAG
HE'S DUG HIM OUT OF SOMEWHERE
HE'S GOT HIM IN THE BAG

(*At the mention of the family solicitor, PARCHESTER, the family solicitor, crosses the balcony from right to left in front of GERALD.*)

   GERALD. (*Continued.*)
I'VE SEEN HIM, I'VE SEEN HIM, HE'S HERE
   ALL. (*Ad lib.*) He's here, he's here!
   GERALD.
AND ALMOST ANY MOMENT
   ALL.
ALMOST ANY MOMENT
   GERALD.
ANY BLESSED MOMENT HE'LL APPEAR
(*GERALD exits balcony, right.*) (ELEC CUE: 7)
   GERALD.
IS HE DARK?
   LADY #2.
IS HE FAIR?
   ALL MEN.
DO YOU THINK WE SHALL CARE
FOR THE NEW LORD HAREFORD?

(*GERALD enters up right and proceeds to make his way down center amid the questioning throng.*)

   LADY #5.
IS HE SHORT?

JAQUIE.
IS HE TALL?
    MAIDS. (*To HETHERSETT.*)
DO YOU THINK WE SHALL FALL
FOR THE NEW LORD HAREFORD?
    ALL MEN.
WON'T YOU TELL US IF YOU CAN
WHAT YOU KNOW ABOUT THE MAN
    MAIDS.
IS HE WHAT WE ALL EXPECT?
    LORD BATTERSBY.
IS HE CIRCUMSPECT?
    LADY BATTERSBY.
IS HE WEAK?
    JAQUIE.
IS HE STRONG?
    HETHERSETT.
DOES HE REALLY BELONG?
    ALL.
IS HE ALL HE SHOULD BE?
    GERALD.
WELL, VERY SOON YOU WILL SEE HIM
    ALL.
VERY, VERY, VERY, VERY SOON
WE SHALL SEE.

(ELEC CUE: 8)

(The party spirit dissolves, and the STAFF begins clearing away some of the plates and empty glasses. The FAMILY, GUEST, and STAFF exit leaving GERALD, JAQUIE, and three STOCKBROKERS. JAQUIE sits on the edge of the left table contemplating her future. The STOCKBROKERS begin paperwork at the right table.)

JAQUIE. So the solicitor's found the heir.
GERALD. (*Center.*) Worse luck for me.
JAQUIE. (*Musing.*) He's going to be a rather rich man, isn't he, Gerald?

GERALD. *(Crosses to JAQUIE.)* Yes. This rather dashes our chances of scooping up the Hareford millions for ourselves, doesn't it?

JAQUIE. Possibly.

GERALD. *(Sits chair, left of JAQUIE.)* Whatever am I going to do?

JAQUIE. Well, you could get a job.

GERALD. I'm sorry?

JAQUIE. You know, work.

GERALD. *(Standing.)* WORK? Jaquie, *Please!* Don't be disgusting. *(He paces center.)* Good lordy. Work! Me? Disgrace the family name? Get up before noon? You must be off your chump. There must be better ways of raising money than that.

(JAQUIE removes her engagement ring and tosses it to GERALD.)

JAQUIE. Well, you could try selling this.

GERALD. But, Jaquie, that's our engagement ring.

JAQUIE. Sorry, darling, I can't afford to mix business with pleasure. If our new Lord Hareford is going to get the money, then I'm going to get our new Lord Hareford.

GERALD. Well, you've bally gone and broken my bally heart. I hope you're satisfied. (ELEC CUE: 9)

[MUSIC CUE #3: THINKING OF NO ONE BUT ME]

GERALD. *(Continued.)*
I ALWAYS IMAGINED THAT WE'D GET ALONG
I STILL HAVE THAT NOTION BUT MAYBE I'M
   WRONG
(He crosses to JAQUIE.)
THE FEMALE EMOTION WILL THRIVE ON—I
   LEARN
A LITTLE INVESTMENT—
   JAQUIE.
—AND PLENTY OF RETURN

(*JAQUIE brushes by GERALD to down center.*)
ME I'M FOR THE TOP OF THE TREE
JUST YOU LOOK UP AND YOU'LL SEE
WHAT'S GOING TO HAPPEN TO ME

I WANT ALL THAT MONEY CAN BUY
I'LL MAKE MY LIMIT THE SKY
THIS IS HOORAY AND GOODBYE
(*JAQUIE flirts and dances with the STOCKBROKERS.*)
WHILE I'M YOUNG AND HEALTHY
I'LL FIND SOMEONE WEALTHY
SOME RICH CITY PRIZE
WITH RINGS ON HIS FINGERS
    GERALD. And under his eyes.
    JAQUIE.
ME -- JUST YOU LOOK UP AND YOU'LL SEE
ME ON THE TOP OF THE TREE
THINKING NOTHING OF NO ONE BUT ME

I'LL MAKE MEN SO FOND THAT THEIR PULSES WILL STIR
AND I'LL BE THE BLONDE THAT THE FELLOWS PREFER
THE PAST THAT I CLUNG TO IS NOW ON THE WING
DON'T CARE WHERE I'M FLUNG TO, I'M GOING TO HAVE MY FLING

ME -- I'M FOR THE TOP OF THE TREE
JUST YOU LOOK UP AND YOU'LL SEE
    GERALD. What's going to happen to me?
    JAQUIE.
I -- WANT ALL THAT MONEY CAN BUY
I'LL MAKE MY LIMIT THE SKY
THIS IS HOORAY AND GOODBYE

WHILE I'M YOUNG AND HEALTHY
I'LL FIND SOMEONE WEALTHY

SOME BIG CITY MAN --
GERALD. Who'll cancel the contract as soon as he can!
JAQUIE.
ME -- JUST YOU LOOK UP AND YOU'LL SEE
ME ON THE TOP OF THE TREE
THINKING NOTHING OF NO ONE
BUT ME! (ELEC CUE: 10)

(THE STOCKBROKERS collect their papers and exit right as LORD BATTERSBY, entering down left, makes for the whiskey decanter on the left buffet table. He is about to pour himself a drink when LADY BATTERSBY enters behind him. JAQUIE and GERALD compose themselves at the right buffet table.)

LADY BATTERSBY. Frederick, not another drop.
LORD BATTERSBY. Certainly, my dear.

(The center doors open and PARCHESTER, briefcase in hand, enters followed by SIR JASPER TRING. He crosses downright, and opens his briefcase. He is set upon by FAMILY members.)

LADY BATTERSBY. Ah, Mr. Parchester.
PARCHESTER. Good afternoon, Lady Battersby, Lord Battersby.
LORD BATTERSBY. What's all this about an heir?
SIR JASPER. *(With ear trumpet.)* Eh?
PARCHESTER. The Duchess is coming. Perhaps we should wait.
LORD BATTERSBY. Who is he?
SIR JASPER. Eh?
LORD BATTERSBY. Where is he?

(JAQUIE notices her mother, MARIA, DUCHESS OF DENE, entering up left and hushes the FAMILY.

MARIA crosses down left center followed by HETHERSETT who sets her chair.)

DUCHESS. Good afternoon, Sir Jasper, Freddy, Clara, Mr. Parchester. Be seated. (*She sits.*) Where is Sir John?

GERALD. (*Crosses to right of DUCHESS.*) I passed him in the hallway trying to recover from the dreadful shock we've all had. (*Continues his cross, left, to the table. He pours himself a drink. SIR JAPSER sits down right, PARCHESTER, right center, The BATTERSBYS stand to the right of the DUCHESS. SIR JOHN TREMAYNE enters down left to the sound of barking dogs. He pours himself a whiskey.*)

SIR JOHN. Dammit it all, Maria, those poodles of yours take an unhealthy interest in my ankles.

DUCHESS. You're late, John.

SIR JOHN. Yes, Maria.

DUCHESS. Sit down.

SIR JOHN. (*Sits left of DUCHESS.*) Yes, Maria.

DUCHESS. Well, now that we're all gathered, Mr. Parchester has some news which affects us all. Parchester.

PARCHESTER. Your Grace. Now you will all be aware that the last Lord Hareford, in his youth, contracted an unfortunate marriage with a most unsuitable young woman.

(*The FAMILY grumbles acknowledgment.*)

PARCHESTER. They soon parted and she died. There were rumours of a son, however, and the late Lord Hareford's will had to provide for the possibility of his one day turning up. I have to tell you all that it is quite certain that he has turned up.

SIR JOHN. Good Lord. So there is a new Lord Hareford.

PARCHESTER. Assuredly, Sir John. However, it is not quite as simple as that. The will insists that the heir must be a person fit and proper to assume his place here.

GERALD. I see. But how do we decide whether he is fit and proper.

PARCHESTER. The two executors of the will must decide, Gerald. Her Grace and Sir John.

SIR JOHN. (*Standing.*) Well, what sort of cricketer is he?

(*Men ad lib "Here, here!"*)

SIR JOHN. (*Pouring himself a drink.*) Well, wheel him in. Let's take a look at him. Ring the bell, Gerald.

PARCHESTER. Well, before he is introduced to you all, I should say...

GERALD. (*Crossing to right to bell ring.*) Come on, Parchester, get on with it.

LORD BATTERSBY. Rather!

SIR JASPER. Eh?

JAQUIE. (*Behind PARCHESTER's chair.*) He agrees. Come along.

LORD BATTERSBY. We are all on absolute tenterhooks, aren't we, my love?

LADY BATTERSBY. Frederic.

LORD BATTERSBY. My Lamb?

LADY BATTERSBY. Shut up! (*The BATTERSBYS cross above the right buffet table. GERALD has returned to the up left side of the left table. PARCHESTER stands.*)

PARCHESTER. But I feel I should tell you that his new Lordship is not, perhaps, quite what...

SIR JOHN. (*Crossing away, down left.*) Damn it all, Parchester, never knew such a fellow for talking.

SIR JASPER. Eh?

(*PARCHESTER, defeated, returns his chair against the right table. As he turns back, center JAQUIE is waiting for him. FOOTMAN enters up left and crosses to the foot of the staircase.)*

JAQUIE. What's he called, Parchester, the new earl?
PARCHESTER. Eh, William is his first name, Lady Jaqueline.
JAQUIE. (*Musing.*) Ah, William.

(DUCHESS and SIR JASPER stand in anticipation of Lord Hareford's entrance. JAQUIE crosses, right, to table. PARCHESTER crosses up left to FOOTMAN.)

PARCHESTER. Show the gentleman in now, please.
LADY BATTERSBY. Does he know yet who he really is?
PARCHESTER. No. I felt it should be broken to him gently.
FOOTMAN. (*Opening doors.*) If you would like to come this way, sir.

(BILL enters. The FAMILY is aghast.)

BILL. Oi! Oi! (*Looking around.*) Bloody 'ell! 'ow do.
PARCHESTER. Welcome to Hareford, William.
BILL. Cheer's Squire! (*BILL pretends to dive down the stairs, collects himself, and struts down center. The FAMILY is in shock. PARCHESTER directs BILL to the DUCHESS.*)
PARCHESTER. May I present Her Grace, the Duchess of Dene.
BILL. (*Shaking her hand vigorously.*) Nice to meet you, lady, very nice indeed.
DUCHESS. (*Sits left, in shock.*) How do you do? May I introduce you to an old friend of the family, Sir John Tremayne.
BILL. (*Crushing SIR JOHN's hand.*) Wotcher, me old cock. Nice to meet you.
SIR JOHN. (*Stares in disbelief.*) Good Lord!

ME AND MY GIRL

DUCHESS. My daughter, Lady Jaqueline Carstone.
JAQUIE. (*Crossing to BILL, hand extended in high fashion.*) How do you do.
BILL. (*Attempted fashion.*) How do you do.
JAQUIE. (*Trying to please.*) Nice to meet you.
BILL. (*A little over amorous.*) Yes, very nice to meet you and all. Very nice.

(*GERALD crosses to BILL's left.*)

DUCHESS. Her fiance, my nephew, Gerald Bolingbroke.
GERALD. How do you do.

(*BILL turns to GERALD and accidently drops his cigarette in GERALD's drink.*)

BILL. How do you...Sorry, I dropped my cigarette in your drink.
GERALD. Oh, how disgusting.

(*GERALD extracts cigarette from glass and returns to left table. BILL is left with the soiled glass in his right hand.*)

DUCHESS. Lord and Lady Battersby.

(*The BATTERSBYS cross from downright to BILL's right. LORD BATTERSBY extends an antique decanter.*)

LORD BATTERSBY. How do you do?
BILL. How are you, my old China? Nice to meet you.
LORD BATTERSBY. I expect you'd like a drink.
BILL. (*Fumbles with decanter.*) Rather!
LORD BATTERSBY. (*In shock.*) Be careful! That decanter is over two hundred years old.

BILL. Thank God for that. It could have been a new one.

(*LORD BATTERSBY takes decanter and glass from BILL. As he crosses left to return glass to table he tries to drink the contents of BILL's glass. LADY BATTERSBY is too sharp for him.*)

LADY BATTERSBY. Frederic!
LORD BATTERSBY. (*Discovered.*) Oh, right-o. (*To BILL.*) Perhaps later, eh?
BILL. That's right, you tell 'im darling. Bit of a lad, is he? (*BILL swats LADY BATTERSBY's rear. She screams in horror and crosses up right. LORD BATTERSBY crosses to her aid.*)
DUCHESS. Mr. Parchester you already know and this is Sir Jasper Tring.
SIR JASPER. Whoozat?
BILL. (*Crosses right to JAPSER. Imaginary sign language.*) Very pleased to meet you, sunshine. (*BILL returns center, to DUCHESS.*) My mates call me Bill.
PARCHESTER. (*Crosses down right center.*) Shall we proceed, Your Grace?
DUCHESS. Sit down, please, William.
BILL. Ta, very much. (*Attempts to sit in chair next to DUCHESS unaware that SIR JOHN has just done the same. He jumps up reproachfully, and sits, center, in a chair provided by PARCHESTER. JAQUIE and BILL sit on this chair simultaneously, and so BILL finds himself uncomfortably close to JAQUIE during the following.*)

DUCHESS. Before we tell you why you are here, we would like to know something about you, William.
SIR JOHN. Where do you live?
BILL. I live in a distant village called London.
JAQUIE. But what part?
BILL. All of me.
GERALD. What part of London, you clot?

BILL. Lambeth.
DUCHESS. Lambeth!
SIR JOHN. Good Lord!
SIR JASPER. Where's Lambeth?
BILL. (*An attempt at "Signing."*) Oi, it's the best part of Lambeth, Squire. Just north of Brixton, just south of ...

(*SIR JASPER interprets BILL's "signing" as a rude gesture and delights in repeating it.*)

GERALD. Oh crumbs.
SIR JOHN. In a house or flat?
BILL. I've got a parlour, drawing room, dining room, kitchen, bathroom, bedroom. All in the same room. 'bout the size of that fireplace over there.

(*The FAMILY squint front attempting to focus on the fireplace at the far end of the room. BILL stands indicating the parts of his body.*)

BILL. The bath's in the sink. One day you bath your top part, the next day you bath your middle part and the third day you bath your...
SIR JOHN. (*Stands.*) What do you live on?
BILL. Me wits.
SIR JOHN. (*Crossing downstage.*) You must be severely undernourished. Now look, what do you actually do?
BILL. (*Crossing to SIR JOHN.*) Do? Anything, Squire. I do a bit of sparring now and again, y'know, run for a bookie, sell fruit off a barrow. (*Crossing to SIR JASPER.*) Olly, olly, all fresh—ripe strawberries...

(*SIR JASPER interprets BILL's "strawberries" as a woman's breast and lewdly repeats the gesture. BILL pulls a deck of cards from his pocket and returns to SIR JOHN.*)

BILL. And I do a bit of quickness that deceives the eyes. Take a card, any card. Do I know this man?

(*The FAMILY comes in for a closer look responding accordingly to the excitement of the moment.*)

BILL. No, I do not know this man. Take a card, any card —go on, go on, go on... (*Under cover of the cards, BILL picks SIR JOHN's pocket of his watch. SIR JOHN takes a card.*) What is it?
SIR JOHN. Five of spades.
BILL. Correct. The man wins a gold watch. (*Hands SIR JOHN his own watch.*)
SIR JOHN. That's my watch. He lifted my watch. Let's just get on with it, shall we? (*Crosses away down left. PARCHESTER steps down to BILL's right.*)
DUCHESS. Now we have a surprise for you, William.
BILL. Oh, yeah?
DUCHESS. Parchester.
PARCHESTER. Your grace. Do you know anything about your parents. William?
BILL. They're brown bread.
GERALD. Brown bread?
DUCHESS. What are you talking about? Brown bread?
BILL. Like I said, brown bread, dead.
GERALD. (*Crossing to BILL's left.*) Oh, it's cockney rhyming slang. I say, can you do that?
SIR JOHN. Rhyming slang?
GERALD. (*Enthusiastically.*) Yes, you hear it all the time at racetracks. (*Recollecting himself.*) Um... apparently...So I've been told. (*Retreats up left.*)
PARCHESTER. You're trying to tell us that your parents are dead?
BILL. Like I said, brown bread. Snuffed it. That is if I had any parents, 'coz I think I was spontaneous. You know what I mean?

ME AND MY GIRL 25

PARCHESTER. Well, not quite. The facts are these. Your late father was the Earl of Hareford. You were his only son. Therefore, William Alexander Henry Charles Augustus Presteigne-Snibson, you are now by right and lawful succession the 18th Baron Haveringland, High Steward of the Brandiston Estuary, Marshall Royal in Ordinary to the Marquisate of Snetterton and the 14th Earl of Hareford.

(All stand. All, but DUCHESS bows. There is a silence. BILL bends down to look up into PARCHESTER's face.)

BILL. Gettaway! You're pulling my tinkler, encha?
SIR JOHN. Nothing could be more serious.

(BILL drops to the floor in a dead faint.)

SIR JOHN. Good Lord, he's fainted. Quick, water.
BILL. *(Reviving.)* "Ere, I didn't faint for water.
SIR JOHN. Brandy, then.

(PARCHESTER and GERALD lift BILL to the center chair. PARCHESTER returns to right position, JAQUIE and GERALD stand behind center chair. BILL drinks from decanter offered by SIR JOHN. DUCHESS stands left of BILL. SIR JOHN crosses away, down left.)

BILL. That'll do, Guv. Cheers. Thanks, Squire.
DUCHESS. This is your family. Your father, the thirteenth Earl, was my brother, You may therefore refer to me as your Aunt Maria. Jaqueline and Gerald are your cousins.
BILL. My family? What him? Nice to meet you, uncle John.
SIR JOHN. *(Revolted.)* Uncle John?
BILL. Ent you and the Duchess married then?

DUCHESS. Good heavens, no.

BILL. Now me a nob, a belted earl. 'Ere, does this mean I've got a lot of bees, then?

PARCHESTER. I'm sorry?

BILL. Bees and honey. Money

PARCHESTER. Well, you have about a hundred thousand pounds...

BILL. Oh well, that's not bad, is it...

PARCHESTER. A year.

BILL. (*Crossing to PARCHESTER.*)Bloody 'ell. Cor, dear, oh dear! Well, I'll take this year's installment and be off then.

PARCHESTER. I'm afraid it's not as simple as that.

DUCHESS. (*Standing.*) You are not allowed to touch the inheritance...

BILL. (*Turning to her.*) The howmuch?

DUCHESS. The money, unless the executors of your father's will, Sir John here and myself, are agreed that you are a fit and proper person to stay on here as master of Hareford. Otherwise, you will receive an annuity to live in retirement.

BILL. Fit and proper? Me, for you lot? Forget it (*BILL returns to PARCHESTER. FAMILY around the DUCHESS imploring her to change her mind.*)

DUCHESS. (*To FAMILY.*) Enough! (*She crosses to BILL.*) I will educate you. I am confident you will learn to rule Hareford.

(*The FAMILY breaks away. The BATTERSBYS up right; SIR JASPER and GERALD, left, to bar area of table; PARCHESTER to the right side of the right table. JAQUIE sits in chair at right table.*)

SIR JOHN. (*Remaining.*) Impossible. Look at him. You can't make a silk purse out of a sow's ear.

DUCHESS. William, I am going to make you into a gentleman. If you do as I bid you, blood will tell.

SIR JOHN. If you don't, blood will flow. (*SIR JOHN crossed up left where GERALD and SIR JASPER have drifted. The DUCHESS escorts BILL up center indicating family portraits.*)
DUCHESS. There have been Harefords here as lords of the manor for seven hundred years. You are the last of the line. You will stay here and perpetuate the family.

(*BILL turns downstage, his left hand too close for JAQUIE to resist.*)

BILL. Perpetuate! Strewth! (*BILL extracts his hand from JAQUIE's grasp. The DUCHESS escorts him downstage.*)
DUCHESS. Instead of one room you will have a hundred, and a dozen bathrooms.
BILL. Wait 'til I show this lot to Sally.

(*ALL turn to look at BILL. JAQUIE stands.*)

JAQUIE. Sally?
BILL. Yeah, she' my girl. She's alf gonna love all this.
DUCHESS. This Sally, is she also from?
BILL. Lambeth? Yeah, 'course.

(*DUCHESS sits, left; SIR JOHN comes center. PARCHESTER crosses to BILL's right.*)

PARCHESTER. I should have, perhaps, mentioned, William, that it is a condition of your father's will that you marry a fit and proper wife.
BILL. No, Sally's fit and proper for me, all right. She come with me in the car. I'll get her in. (*He puts his fingers in his mouth and emits a piercing whistle.*)
SIR JOHN. Don't do that.

BILL. All right, calm down. I'll go fetch her in. (*As BILL heads for the door he presents SIR JOHN with his watch again.*)

SIR JOHN. (*Crossing down left.*) He took it again.

DUCHESS. Just one moment. The will states you must marry someone of your own class.

BILL. (*On center stairs.*) That's all right then, 'cos Sally is my own class.

DUCHESS. Not any longer. You may bring her in and tell her who you really are, and then the car will take her back to London.

BILL. Oh yeah? We'll see about that, me old fruit. (*Strawberry gesture to SIR JASPER and BILL is out the door.*) Oi, Sal!

DUCHESS. Well!

SIR JOHN. (*Crossing to DUCHESS.*) I can just see the newspaper headlines. "Hareford's Cockney Lord, fish and chips in the library." Good lord, Maria, you can't let him take over this house.

DUCHESS. It's his birthright. He was born to be an Earl.

SIR JOHN. Yes, but he was brought up to be a wastrel, an idler, and a layabout.

DUCHESS. (*Stands to face SIR JOHN.*) And what is the difference? (*DUCHESS crosses to right chair. SIR JOHN stands in front of lower left chair; LORD BATTERSBY in front of upper left chair with LADY BATTERSBY behind. GERALD is in front of down right chair, JAQUIE behind him. PARCHESTER observes the FAMILY from up right center.*)

SIR JOHN. Can you imagine what his girlfriend will be like?

DUCHESS. John, if our King chooses to abdicate for some colonial woman, that is one thing, but I am not allowing a member of this family to do the same.

SIR JOHN. But what are we to do?

DUCHESS. Mr. Parchester is here to advise.

ME AND MY GIRL

GERALD. Yes, dear Mr. Parchester, please do advise. (ELEC CUE: 11)

(PARCHESTER moves center. GERALD, DUCHESS, LORD BATTERSBY, and SIR JOHN sit on music cue.)

[MUSIC CUE #4: THE FAMILY SOLICITOR]

PARCHESTER.
AS THE FAMILY SOLICITOR
HERE'S MY ADVICE TO YOU
AS THE FAMILY SOLICITOR
HERE'S WHAT YOU OUGHT TO DO
FOR SIX AND EIGHT I'LL PUT YOU STRAIGHT
WHEN ANYTHING GOES WRONG
FOR I CONTEND YOU MUST PRETEND
THAT LIFE IS ONE SWEET SONG

SO SING A LITTLE AND DANCE A LITTLE
BE GAY A LITTLE AND PLAY A LITTLE
BRING YOUR TROUBLES MORE AND MORE
TO THE FAMILY SOLICITOR

SAY A LITTLE AND THINK A LITTLE
AND EAT A LITTLE AND DRINK A LITTLE
KEEP A DROP OF THE NINETY-FOUR
FOR THE FAMILY SOLICITOR

HE'LL TAKE ALL YOUR CASES
KEEP YOU IN YOUR PLACES
MAYBE SAVE YOUR FACES
HA! HA! HA! HA! HA! HA! HA!

HOP A LITTLE AND SKIP A LITTLE
AND JUMP A LITTLE, LET RIP A LITTLE
THANK YOUR LUCKY STARS ONCE MORE
FOR THE FAMILY, THE FAMILY

THE FAMILY SOLICITOR

DUCHESS.
HE'LL TAKE ALL YOUR CASES
KEEP US IN OUR PLACES
　SIR JOHN.
MAYBE SAVE YOUR FACES
　FAMILY.
HA! HA! HA! HA! HA! HA! HA!
SING A LITTLE AND DANCE A LITTLE
BE GAY A LITTLE AND PLAY A LITTLE
BRING YOUR TROUBLES MORE AND MORE
TO THE FAMILY SOLICITOR
　PARCHESTER.
SAY A LITTLE AND THINK A LITTLE
AND EAT A LITTLE AND DRINK A LITTLE
KEEP A DROP OF THE NINETY-FOUR
FOR THE FAMILY SOLICITOR
HE'LL TAKE ALL YOUR CASES
KEEP YOU IN YOUR PLACES
MAYBE SAVE YOUR FACES
HA! HA! HA! HA!
　PARCHESTER AND WOMEN.
HA! HA! HA! HA!
　ALL MEN.
HA! HA! HA! HA! HA! HA! HA! HA!

HOP A LITTLE AND SKIP A LITTLE
AND JUMP A LITTLE, LET RIP A LITTLE
　MEN OF THE FAMILY.
THANK YOUR LUCKY STARS ONCE MORE
FOR THE FAMILY SOLICITOR
　PARCHESTER.
HOP A LITTLE AND SKIP A LITTLE
AND JUMP A LITTLE, LET RIP A LITTLE
THANK YOUR LUCKY STARS ONCE MORE
FOR THE FAMILY SOLICITOR

ME AND MY GIRL

FAMILY.
HOP A LITTLE AND SKIP A LITTLE
AND JUMP A LITTLE, LET RIP A LITTLE
THANK YOUR LUCKY STARS ONCE MORE
MEN.
FOR THE FAMILY
WOMEN.
HA! HA! HA! HA! HA! HA! HA!
MEN OF THE FAMILY.
THE FAMILY
WOMEN.
HA! HA! HA! HA! HA! HA! HA!
FAMILY.
FOR THE FAMILY SOLICI...
PARCHESTER.
TOR...
FAMILY.
THE FAMILY SOLICITOR
THE FAMILY SOLICITOR
THE FAMILY SOLICITOR
PARCHESTER.
THE FAMILY SOLICITOR   (ELEC CUE: 12)

(HETHERSETT and STAFF enter. They set the buffet tables horizontally, and remove all items except candelabras, champagne bucket, newspaper, pheasant, candy dish, fruit bowl, and liquor bottles. Chairs are arranged to suit the scene.)

DUCHESS. *(Breaking left.)* I shall go for a walk in the rose garden to compose myself. *(The DUCHESS exits. The FAMILY crowds around PARCHESTER, down center.)*

GERALD. Thank you very much for that useless advise, Parchester, it's the poorhouse for the lot of us.

SIR JOHN. Dammit, there must be something we can do. Maria must be stopped. I want that man out of this house.

PARCHESTER. Well, we could examine the original will, I suppose.
SIR JOHN. See if we can't find some way out?
FAMILY. (*Ad lib.*)Good idea!
SIR JOHN. Some loophole?

(*FAMILY ad lib response.*)

SIR JOHN. Where is the will?
PARCHESTER. In the library.
SIR JOHN. Then what are we waiting for? The library.

(*FAMILY and STAFF exit. SIR JASPER is the last out.*)

SIR JASPER. Wait for me.   (ELEC CUE: 13)

(*After a moment, the front door opens. BILL pokes his head round.*)

BILL. It's all right, they've all gone. Come in, open your eyes, and clock this.

(*SALLY enters, nervously looking around her.*)

SALLY. Cor blimey! It's the bleedin' Ritz.
BILL. Hear, watch you language, my girl. (*Crossing down to tables.*) Would you care to dine with me Miss Smith. (*He hands his jacket over the back of the left dining chair. SALLY slowly moves down to the tables.*)
SALLY. Oh, Bill, it's 'uge. It's bigger than the British Museum.
BILL. It's cleaner and all. You could eat your dinner off that floor.
SALLY. (*Holds up a copy of the London Times.*) You don't have to. They've even got posh newspapers to eat your chips out of.

BILL. (*Lifts a large port decanter.*) Sal, look at the size of these vinegar bottles.

SALLY. (*Eyes pheasant and wraps it in newspaper to take with her.*) Bill, I still can't believe it.

BILL. It's true. My aunt's a duchess. You know what that makes me?

SALLY. Dutch!

BILL. No. (*Indicating portraits.*) I'm one of them. I'm a lord.

SALLY. And this is your house?

BILL. (*Sits left dining chair.*) My house. Well, our house. (*SALLY sits right dining chair.*) I know, not very 'omely is it?

SALLY. Oh, I'll change all that when we're married. I'll clear out all this old rubbish...and that old armour.

BILL. (*Stands, crosses center.*) Bung up a nice bit of flowered wallpaper, or something.

SALLY. (*Joining BILL.*) Yeah! Shove in some new furniture, net curtains, bit of linoleum. (*Sitting on table.*) Bill, we'll have a lovely motor car.

BILL. (*Sits beside her.*) Not 'alf. You'll be me...What's an earl's wife called?

SALLY. Earless?

BILL. Yeah, you'll be my earless.

SALLY. Bill, when I'm an earless I won't have to work in the fish market no more. And I'll be able to have a little dress shop! I've always wanted a little dress shop.

BILL. Leave it out, girl, you won't have to work.

SALLY. I could have me 'air permed.

BILL. You could have your fingers manacled.

SALLY. And my toes chiropdized, and, Bill, you'll buy me lots of scent.

BILL. 'Course I will. We'll get rid of that fish smell somehow, girl.

SALLY. And when I smell luscious we can go in the three and sixpenny seats in the cinema, 'stead of the one and three pennies.

BILL. Coo, it's a dream, innit? (*BILL stands and crosses a few steps, right.*) 'Ere, I've got to be ejercated.

SALLY. Ejercated? Who says?

BILL. (*Returning.*) Who says? What do you mean who says? The executors. That's my aunt and Sir John.

SALLY. Are they the executors?

BILL. Yeah, not 'alf. They'll chop off the dough if I don't come up scratch. I got a lot to learn, girl. I gotta work fast, do a lot of perpetuating.

SALLY. (*Standing.*) Oh yeah? And where do I fit in?

BILL. What d'you mean?

SALLY. I mean, am I going to be staying here as well?

BILL. Perhaps you could stay at the pub nearby for a few nights. (*SALLY turns away. BILL pursues.*) That duchess, she's a bit of a dragon, she is. We'll sort something out.

SALLY. (*Turning back.*) Bill, all this ain't going to part us, is it?

BILL. What are you taking about? Nothing's going to part me and my girl.

SALLY. If they made you marry one of their lot, I'd die an old maid.

BILL. Hey, Sal, I couldn't live without you.

SALLY. And I couldn't live without you, Bill.

BILL. You're all I've got.   (ELEC CUE:14)

[MUSIC CUE #5: ME AND MY GIRL]

BILL.
LIFE'S AN EMPTY THING
LIFE CAN BE SO AWFUL LONESOME
IF YOUR ALWAYS ON YOUR OWNSOME
LIFE'S AN EMPTY THING
SALLY.
LIFE'S A DIFFERENT THING
WHEN YOU'VE FOUND YOUR ONE AND ONLY
THEN YOU FEEL NO LONGER LONELY

ME AND MY GIRL

LIFE'S A HAPPY THING
> BILL.

EVERYTHING WAS TOPSY-TURVY
LIFE SEEMED ALL WRONG
BUT IT CAME ALL RIGHT AS SOON AS
YOU CAME ALONG

ME AND MY GIRL, MEANT FOR EACH OTHER
SENT FOR EACH OTHER, AND LIKING IT SO
ME AND MY GIRL, IT'S NO USE PRETENDING
WE KNEW THE ENDING A LONG TIME AGO
SOME LITTLE CHURCH, WITH A BIG STEEPLE
JUST A FEW PEOPLE THAT BOTH OF US KNOW
AND WE'LL HAVE LOVE--LAUGHTER
BE HAPPY EVER AFTER, ME AND MY GIRL
> SALLY.

I LOVE TO HEAR YOU SAYING --
ME AND MY GIRL, MEANT FOR EACH OTHER
SENT FOR EACH OTHER, AND LIKING IT SO
ME AND MY GIRL, 'S' NO USE PRETENDING
WE KNEW THE ENDING A LONG TIME AGO
> BOTH.

SOME LITTLE CHURCH,WITH A BIG STEEPLE
JUST A FEW PEOPLE THAT BOTH OF US KNOW
AND WE'LL HAVE LOVE -- LAUGHTER
BE HAPPY EVER AFTER, ME AND MY GIRL

(ELEC CUE: 15)

(Tap break. Ends with BOTH dancing on tables.)

(ELEC CUE: 16)

> BOTH

AND WE'LL HAVE LOVE -- LAUGHTER
BE HAPPY EVER AFTER, ME AND MY GIR...

(ELEC CUE: 17)

(They attempt to kiss, but fall off the back of the tables instead. Heads pop back on tables for musical button. Enter HETHERSETT, MAJOR DOMO and FOOTMEN. BILL and SALLY duck behind the table. DOMO and FOOTMEN line up down left,

HETHERSETT crosses right of center and lifts the tablecloth. BILL and SALLY are discovered.)

HETHERSETT. Good afternoon, my Lord.
BILL. Er, watcher cock. How you doin', all right?
SALLY. *(Indicating FOOTMEN.)* Are they waxworks?
BILL. No, they're usherettes.
SALLY. It is the bleeding Ritz.
HETHERSETT. I am Hethersett, your lordship's butler. May I, on behalf of the staff, welcome you to Hareford, my Lord?
SALLY. Lumme. Bill, Bill, he called you "my Lord."
BILL. *(To SALLY.)* I know. I know. Leave it with me *(Lifts his pant legs as he curtsies.)* Er, thank you very much, thank you. *(Suspects his error and corrects himself.)* Cheers, guv. This is Sally.
SALLY. *(Taking her cue from BILL, lifts her skirts above her knees as she curtsies.)* Pleased to meet you. I'm sure, ever so.

(Embarrassed, BILL brushes her skirt down.)

HETHERSETT. Aperitif, my Lord?
BILL. Eh?
HETHERSETT. Aperitif.
BILL. *(Pointing to his teeth.)* No thanks, I got me own.
HETHERSETT. *(Setting FOOTMAN in action.)* A glass of wine, Miss?
BILL. You haven't got a cigarette, have you?
HETHERSETT. A cigarette? Certainly, my Lord. *(Opens and offers cigarette box to BILL. A FOOTMAN pours two glasses of wine and, during the following, presents them on a tray to SALLY. She takes both; downs one, then the other.)*
BILL. Cheers, Squire. Can Sally 'ave one an' all?
HETHERSETT. They are all yours, my Lord.

ME AND MY GIRL

BILL. Eh?

HETHERSETT. Everything here is the property of your Lordship.

BILL. Oh, Sal...Take the whole boxful. (*He takes a handful of cigarettes and gives them to SALLY who must down the drinks quickly and set the glasses down in order to take the cigarettes. Mild protest.*) Sally. Take the bleedin' box, then. (*He gives the box to SALLY who proceeds to stuff it in her pocket.* [MUSIC CUE #5A: BUNG IT IN THE CAR]) Well, it's all mine now, innit? 'ere what about something for your lodgings in Lambeth? Oi! A cumfy chair. (*BILL picks up a chair and tosses it to a FOOTMAN.*) Bung it in the car, Horace. (*The FOOTMAN exits up center with the chair.*)

SALLY. (*Right, at letter rack.*) Bill, I've always wanted a toast-rack, could I have this?

BILL. 'Course you can.

(*SALLY presents HETHERSETT with a letter rack. BILL picks up candy dish and motions to a second FOOTMAN.*)

BILL. You'll need your hat an' all. Bung it in the Morris, Horace.

(*FOOTMAN exits up center with "hat" from BILL and letter-rack from HETHERSETT. BILL and SALLY in front of armour. BILL pulls sword from armour.*)

BILL. You'll need this in case anyone tries to rob you. (*Giving sword to third FOOTMAN.*) Bung that in the Ford, Claude.

SALLY. (*Pulling on armour.*) And I think I'll take the rest of it for our honeymoon.

(*The suit of armour falls from it's stand and comes to life. Fourth FOOTMAN approaches, but armour exists on it's own legs. FOOTMAN follows. BILL,*

SALLY, HETHERSETT, and MAJOR DOMO are gobsmacked.)

BILL. *(To HETHERSETT.)* Are you sure all this is mine?
HETHERSETT. Everything here is the property of your Lordship.
BILL. Don't argue with the man, Sal. Let's grab all this stuff. *(BILL and SALLY gather items from the table and begin to exit up center.)*
HETHERSETT. Would you care for a box, my Lord?
BILL. A box? Don't be daft. I got enough to carry as it is. (ELEC CUE: 18)

[MUSIC CUE #6: AN ENGLISH GENTLEMAN]

(BILL and SALLY stare at each other as lights fade and scene changes to the cellar kitchens of HAREFORD HALL.) (CREW CUE: 6)

Scene 2

The kitchen.
Upstage left, by the entrance, various pots and pans are boiling away on the kitchen range. Upstage Right stands the kitchen sink by the dumb waiter. The two buffet tables from the previous scene have been stripped of their clothes, and are now plain deal tables.
The STAFF and SERVANTS are gathered in the kitchen, where HETHERSETT directs them in the preparation of a meal for the HAREFORD FAMILY.

(ELEC CUE: 19)

HETHERSETT & STAFF.
WILLIAM OF HAREFORD IS DIAMETRICALLY
IN REALITY, THEORETICALLY

QUITE OPPOSED, AND THAT PATHETICALLY
TO ALL THAT APPERTAINS TO GENTLE FOLK

SO WE FACE WITH GREAT DUBIETY
THIS SAD LACK OF PURE PROPRIETY
HE'S NO SENSE OF HIGH SOCIETY
THE FELLOW EVEN CALLS HIMSELF A BLOKE
    HETHERSETT.
HE TAKES HIS FOOD WITH A HORRID ZEST
HE EATS ONE HALF AND HE WEARS THE REST
    WOMEN STAFF.
THOUGH IT MAY BE TRUE THAT HIS BLOOD IS BLUE
    CHEF.
IT IS NOTHING LIKE AS PURPLE AS HIS LANGUAGE
(*He whispers to the PARLOURMAID, who drops the plate she is holding.*)
    ALL.
HE'S ROUGH, HE'S CRUDE, HE'S TOUGH, HE'S RUDE
BY ALL OF US IT'S UNDERSTOOD
HE'LL NEVER MAKE THE NOBLE RAKE
THAT CONSTITUTES A GENTLEMAN, AN ENGLISH GENTLEMAN

(*The bell rings and HETHERSETT and the UPSTAIRS STAFF exit briefly, then return with the news.*)

    MAJOR DOMO & FOOTMAN.
WE SERVED HIM PEAS AND THEY ALL SHOT FORTH
    MAID #1.
TO THE EAST
    MAID #2.
AND WEST
    MAID #1.
TO THE SOUTH

MAID #2.
AND NORTH
MAJOR DOMO.
THEN HE LET ONE FLY AND IT STRUCK THE EYE
OF LADY MARGARET LEICESTER
ALL.
POOR LADY "M," WHAT A FEARFUL BORE
SHE'S NEVER HAD A PEA IN HER EYE BEFORE
HE'S ROUGH, HE'S CRUDE, HE'S TOUGH, HE'S RUDE
BY ALL OF US IT'S UNDERSTOOD
HE'LL NEVER MAKE THE NOBLE RAKE
THAT CONSTITUTES A GENTLEMAN, AN ENGLISH GENTLEMAN
AN ENGLISH GENTLE...

(Enter BILL in riding habit, walking bow-legged. He whistles for attention.) (ELEC CUE: 20)

BILL. Oi! Give us a beer, Charlie.

(The SERVANTS are terrified and embarrassed at BILL's unorthodox entrance and demand. HETHERSETT claps his hands to an UNDERLING, who fetches the beer.)

HETHERSETT. Pleasant ride, my Lord?
BILL. Pleasant ride? I'm gonna have to put that horse on a diet. It'll take me a week to straighten out these legs.

(The COOK crosses downstage.)

BILL. Dear, oh dear, what's this?
COOK. It's bean soup.
BILL. I don't care what it's been, what is it now?
MAJOR DOMO. Her Grace thinks your Lordship is too convivial with us.

BILL. Too convivial...Well, she's not going to come down here, is she?

HETHERSETT. Indeed not, my Lord, Your Lordship is the first member of the family ever to have been down here.

BILL. Do what?

HETHERSETT. It is quite unheard of, my Lord.

BILL. (*Crossing up left, behind tables.*) What's the matter with you lot? Cor blimey, the family looks down at me and you lot look up at me. (*Passes behind a MAID. Startled by his obvious pinch, she mistakenly slaps the face of a FOOTMAN at her left. BILL ignores the chaos. Sits center.*) I'm 'emmed in like a 'am in a sandwich. I think I'll go down to the old rub a dub dub.

HETHERSETT. The what, Sir?

BILL. It's a pub. See if Sally's all right.

HETHERSETT. Her Grace does not approve of your visiting Miss Smith in the rub a dub dub.

BILL. I dunno. The King never 'ad this trouble, did 'e? One quick speech on the wireless and 'e and 'is missus were shot o' the lot of them. I know just how he felt, now.

[MUSIC CUE #6A: AN ENGLISH GENTLEMAN
(Reprise)]

MAID. I overheard Her Grace sayin' she intends to part you and Miss Sally, my Lord.

BILL. (*Standing.*) Infamy! Infamy! They've all got it in-fa-me! (*Sits, painfully. The STAFF clears the kitchen behind the SERVANT's chorus. As the SERVANTS exit we find ourselves in the drawing room of Hareford.*) (ELEC CUE: 21)

SERVANTS. (CREW CUE: 7)
BY ALL OF US IT'S UNDERSTOOD
HE'LL NEVER MAKE THE NOBLE RAKE

THAT CONSTITUTES A GENTLEMAN, AN ENGLISH
  GENTLEMAN
THAT CONSTITUTES A GENTLEMAN, AN ENGLISH
  GENTLEMAN

Scene 3

The drawing room.
The scene is backed by the drawing room windows, overlooking the grounds.
The FOOTMEN deliver a small Chesterfield to Stage Right and a desk and chair to Stage Left.
BILL walks gingerly to the sofa and sits. JAQUIE enters unbeknownst to BILL, and perches on the arm of the sofa. BILL rests his elbow on the arm of the sofa, and unwittingly puts his hand on JAQUIE's thigh.

(ELEC CUE: 22)

BILL. Oh my Gawd!
JAQUIE. Well, here we are again.
BILL. Yes, I'm seeing rather a lot of you lately.

(JAQUIE stands and crosses in front of BILL to sit at his right.)

JAQUIE. I thought we might meet this morning as Mummy has suggested I take you in hand. (*She sits on his hand.*) To teach you about art and literature and life.
  BILL. (*Extracting his hand.*) Oh ah.
  JAQUIE. (*Crossing her legs.*) Bill, there's so much I want to show you.
  BILL. (*Eyeing her legs.*) Yes, I can see that. (*BILL tries to cross his legs, but horse riding has made that too painful. He grimaces. JAQUIE extends her hand to assist. BILL jumps to the arm of the sofa where he perches with an air of nonchalance.*)
  JAQUIE. How familiar are you with our great writers and painters and poets? Do you like Kipling?

ME AND MY GIRL

BILL. (*Sliding beside her.*) I dunno, I've never Kipled.

JAQUIE. (*New attack.*) Bill, you and I are soul mates. I can look deep into your eyes and see what you're thinking.

BILL. Then why don't you slap my face?

JAQUIE. (*Hand behind his neck.*) You're a man.

BILL. This is true.

JAQUIE. (*Pulling him to her.*) I'm a woman.

BILL. My gawd! So you are.

JAQUIE. (*Turning out.*) I can see it all so clearly.

BILL. Not as clearly as I can, girl.

JAQUIE. I'm sailing away with you. I'm abroad.

BILL. You certainly are.

JAQUIE. To Italy. Ah, Florence! Beautiful Florence, just we two, making love.

BILL. What, you and Florence?

JAQUIE. (*Turning to BILL.*) You kiss me on the piazza.

BILL. So, I missed.

JAQUIE. Bill, it's useless to resist. Can't you feel my heart pounding? (*She takes his hand and places it on her bosom.*)

BILL. (*Jumping away.*) Oi! Oi! Oi! Don't start all that. Cor strewth! Someone might come in.

JAQUIE. Let them come in, Bill. Let the whole world come in. What have I got to hide?

BILL. Well...There's...and...thingy!

JAQUIE. Oh, Bill, if only you knew how long I've been waiting for you.

[MUSIC CUE #7: YOU WOULD IF YOU COULD]

BILL. Get off, I was only downstairs.

(ELEC CUE: 23)

JAQUIE.
HOW I'VE LOOKED FOR SOMEONE WHO
PLAYS UPON MY HEART LIKE YOU

TALL AND DARK AND HANDSOME--AND SWEET
SOMEONE WHO WOULD TAKE MY HEART
MAYBE TEAR MY SOUL APART
SEE, I LAY MYSELF AT YOUR FEET

YOU WOULD IF YOU COULD
YOU COULD AND YOU SHOULD
AND YOU WOULD IF YOU COULD.
    BILL. But I can't.
    JAQUIE.
I'M SURE THAT YOU CAN
I KNOW THAT YOU'RE A MAN
AND YOU WOULD IF YOU COULD
    BILL. But I shan't.
    JAQUIE.
WHEN YOU'RE A BAD BOY
YOU GO MY WAY
BUT YOU'RE A GOOD BOY
AND SO YOU SAY -- REGRETFULLY

YOU WOULD IF YOU COULD
YOU COULD AND YOU SHOULD
AND YOU WOULD IF YOU COULD
    BILL. No, it's impossible.
I MIGHT PUT MY ARMS AROUND YOU
DO THE THINGS THAT MOST MEN DO
MEN NOT SO HIGH-MINDED AS I
I CAN'T DO THAT CAVEMAN STUFF
SOCK 'EM HARD, TREAT 'EM ROUGH
MOTHER WOULDN'T LIKE ME TO TRY
    JAQUIE.
YOU WOULD IF YOU COULD
YOU COULD AND YOU SHOULD
AND YOU WOULD IF YOU COULD
    BILL. But, I don't.
    JAQUIE.
I'M SURE THAT YOU DO
JUST LOOK AT THE VIEW

AND YOU WOULD IF YOU COULD
 BILL. But, I won't.
 JAQUIE.
YOU'RE LIKE AN APPLE ON TOP OF A TREE
I'D LIKE TO SHAKE YOU
I'D LIKE TO SEE YOU FALLING FOR ME
 BILL.
I WOULD IF I COULD
 JAQUIE.
BILL -- YOU COULD AND YOU SHOULD
AND YOU WOULD IF YOU COULD -- BILL

(BILL is about to give in to JAQUIE's seduction when SALLY and GERALD rush on from left. BILL sees SALLY.)

BILL. I really think it's out of the question.
(ELEC CUE: 24)
(BILL falls behind the sofa. JAQUIE composes herself. GERALD is beside himself with what he thinks is rage.)
GERALD. Jaquie!
JAQUIE. Hello, Gerald.
GERALD. Hello, Gerald?
SIR JASPER. Just giving William an etiquette lesson.
GERALD. Really? Jaquie, I'm shocked. I'm astonished. I'm amazed. I'm a startled person.
JAQUIE. *(Had enough.)* Gerald, do you mind?
GERALD. Yes, I do mind. I'm staggered and jiggered and profoundly disturbed. I am going upstairs to bathe my temples in eau de cologne. *(Exits, left. BILL comes up from behind the sofa.)*
BILL. Oh, 'ello, Sal.
SALLY. Bill, would you 'ave the goodness to present my compliments to Lady Jaqueline and tell her I would like to have converse with you alone.

JAQUIE. (*Standing.*) William, please tell Miss Smith I was just leaving. I detect an odour of prudishness in the room.

SALLY. The smell to what 'er Ladyness is referring, William, seems to come from some cheap French scent in the neighbourhood of that settee.

JAQUIE. (*Crossing to SALLY.*) Perhaps Miss Smith is not aware, William, that such gross impertinence betrays her obvious lace of breeding.

SALLY. Thank 'er Ladyship for me, William, and tell her that if I want lessons in her kind of breeding, I can go to a farmyard.

JAQUIE. How dare you!

BILL. Ohh! Cock-a-doodle-do!

JAQUIE. William, I'll see you later, when your little friend has gone.

SALLY. That's right, dear, you run off and sew up your dress.

(*JAQUIE exits, left, in high dudgeon. BILL crosses to SALLY.*)

BILL. Ohh! Saucer of milk for Miss Smith.

SALLY. She don't 'alf get my dander up, that one.

BILL. I know what you mean, girl. She got mine...How's my girl?

SALLY. (*Crossing right, repelling his advances.*) I'm fed up staying at the pub. I don't like coming round here, the duchess don't want me.

BILL. (*Crossing toward her.*) The duchess? This is my house. If you go, I go.

SALLY. No, she's right, Bill. As long as I'm around, you can't grow into a gentleman.

BILL. Eh?

SALLY. (*Sits on sofa.*) You'd best forget me.

BILL. Forget you? Forget you? I could no more forget you than I could forget ... uh....uh...   (ELEC CUE: 25)

ME AND MY GIRL

[MUSIC CUE #8: HOLD MY HAND]

BILL.
YOU REQUIRE A LOT OF LOOKING AFTER
THAT'S A JOB IN WHICH I TAKE A PRIDE
SALLY.
YOU CAN ALWAYS MAKE ME SMILE
MAKE MY JOURNEY SEEM WORTHWHILE
BILL.
WHY NOT KEEP ME ALWAYS AT YOUR SIDE
TO GUIDE YOU
HOLD MY HAND
NO MATTER WHAT THE WEATHER
JUST YOU HOLD ME HAND
WE'LL WALK THROUGH LIFE TOGETHER
FOR YOU'LL FIND IN ME
THAT KIND OF FRIEND
SALLY.
WHO WILL SEE ME THROUGH TO THE END
SO IF YOU'LL HOLD MY HAND
WE BOTH SHALL WALK MORE STEADILY
BILL.
FOR UNDERSTAND
YOU HOLD MY HEART ALREADY
IN THAT DREAMLAND WHERE I HAVE PLANNED
BILL AND SALLY.
THAT I SHALL HOLD YOUR HAND FOREVER

(ELEC CUE: 26)

(JAQUIE enters with CRICKET and TENNIS PLAYERS. MEN pull BILL from SALLY and dress him in cricket gear to JAQUIE's delight. SALLY rushes out up center. BILL follows. JAQUIE exits.)

["HOLD MY HAND" dance extension.]

(ELEC CUE: 27)

(DUCHESS enters from down right followed by SIR JOHN and PARCHESTER. She crosses right center to address the PLAYERS.)

DUCHESS. If you're going to play, play outside.

(PLAYERS exit up center. DUCHESS crosses to desk. SIR JOHN follows.)

SIR JOHN. Maria, why are you persisting with this nonsense? Nothing you can do or say will convince me that William could be made remotely fit or proper for Hareford.
DUCHESS. *(Crossing to sofa.)* We shall see. I have sent for him.
SIR JOHN. *(Crossing to sofa.)* You and I used to understand each other.
DUCHESS. Sir John...
SIR JOHN. *(Advancing, sits to her left.)* Remember when we were young? I used to climb that old cherry tree in your father's orchard. I'd throw down all the best fruit for you.
DUCHESS. And we'd eat until we felt sick.
SIR JOHN. We were very close in those days.

(PARCHESTER has crossed to behind the desk during the previous moment. Suddenly the center doors fly open and two FOOTMEN enter carrying BILL.)

BILL. I am the Earl of Hareford. I could have you boys thrown in the Tower. Put me down.

(FOOTMEN drop him and exit up center.)

DUCHESS. Thank you for dropping by. It's time for some more lessons.
BILL. *(Standing in protest.)* I was just going down to the pub to see if Sally is all right.
SIR JOHN. *(Standing.)* Maria...
DUCHESS. I hope you don't mean to thwart me, John.
BILL. Go on, John Give her a good thwarting.

DUCHESS. You may leave us, Sir John. We have work to do.

SIR JOHN. (*Starts left.*) Back to my kennel.

BILL. (*Stops him and presents watch.*) Here you are, John.

SIR JOHN. (*Exiting left.*) Thank you...Choc! That's my watch...

DUCHESS. Parchester....

PARCHESTER. Yes, your Grace.

BILL. (*Crosses to right of PARCHESTER.*) What's today's torture, then?

PARCHESTER. I felt we should begin with your personal correspondence.

BILL. Oi, Oi, fan mail. What do they all want, then?

PARCHESTER. Well, this one, for instance, is from Celia Worthington-Worthington. She wants to know if you'll lay the foundation stone for the new hospital.

BILL. Celia Worthington-Worthington? I don't even know her-know her.

DUCHESS. The Worthington-Worthingtons are one of the oldest families in England.

BILL. Then tell her I'll do it-do it. Here, they're not older than the Harefords?

PARCHESTER. No. Your family pre-dates them by some hundred or so years.

BILL. (*Tearing up the letter.*) Upstarts, social climbers, parvenus! I'll turn them down, down. What's this one here, here?

PARCHESTER. This is a letter asking if you would help the Old Ladies Home.

BILL. Blimey! I didn't know they were still out. (*Picking up a letter off the pile.*) I know this writing. This is a letter from my old mate, Bob Barking. (*BILL crosses downstage. PARCHESTER follows.*) Oi, Oi, good old Bobby! Listen to this: "Dear My Lord, this is to thank you for your wedding present of that bracelet. My missus is very proud of it and wears is on her P.T.O."

(PARCHESTER indicates a page-turning gesture.)

BILL. Oh, wrist.

PARCHESTER. No, no. P.T.O. It stands for please turn over.

BILL. *(Turning letter over.)* "And wears it on her wrist! We thank you for your invite, but we cannot accept because you are not in our class anymore." Marvelous, innit? I'm not in his class. I'm not in your class, Cederico. *(Indicating DUCHESS.)* I'm not in her class. I'm in no class anymore. "We 'ave moved into a new 'ome near the gas works, so there is always a 'orrible smell from your old pal, Bob."

PARCHESTER. *(Back to behind the desk.)* Come along, William, we've got more important things to attend to.

BILL. *(Following.)* What'll I do with this lot, Cedrico?

PARCHESTER. Do you want my advice?

[MUSIC CUE #8A: THE FAMILY SOLICITOR (1st REPRISE)]

BILL. Not 'alf.

PARCHESTER. *(Pulling flower from vase.)* Well,
AS THE FAMILY SOLICITOR
HERE'S MY ADVICE TO YOU
AS THE FAMILY SOLICITOR...

DUCHESS. That'll do, Parchester. You may leave us.

PARCHESTER. Your Grace. *(PARCHESTER exists left. DUCHESS crosses to BILL.)*

DUCHESS. Now, William, I have come to a decision. It is time local society had a chance to meet you. Tongues have wagged for long enough. To that end I have issued invitations to a party to be held in honor of your succession.

BILL. *(Showing letter.)* That means my old friend, Bob Barking, can come.

ME AND MY GIRL

DUCHESS. No. It will be a select gathering of the county. (*DUCHESS crosses down left.*) Now let us go over our previous lessons. "Good afternoon, Lord Hareford."

(*BILL crosses center, assumes a pose in gross exaggeration of a proper gentleman, and staggers, left, to the DUCHESS.*)

BILL. Oh I say, dash it and toodle pip and all that rot. I'm going upstairs to bathe my temples in -- eau do you do.
DUCHESS. Eau do you do?
BILL. (*Shaking hands vigorously.*) Very well, thank you. 'Ow do you do? James, put the rolls in the garage. I'll butter them later. It don't 'alf put your neck muscles talking like that. No wonder the upper classes ain't got no chins. (*Crosses to the sofa and lies down. The DUCHESS crosses center.*)
DUCHESS. Yes, well, speaking like a gentleman is one thing, behaving like one is quite another. Already you have broken twelve major and thirty-six minor rules of conduct. Here are a few simple don'ts: (*Throughout the following catalogue of vices, BILL endeavors to correct each one as it is described. This causes him to break another in doing so.*) Don't lie down in my presence. Don't sit while I am standing. Don't wear your hat indoors. Don't smoke without my permission. Don't have the last button of your waistcoat done up. Don't pick up cigarette ends. Don't put your hands in your pockets. Don't slouch, don't sulk and, above all, don't lose your self-control.

(*In utter frustration, BILL dives into the sofa, rolls over the length of it, and finishes standing at the other end wearing his bowler.*)

DUCHESS. Now, most important: When you are the host of the evening, you must go out amongst your guests, the life and soul of the party. Watch me.

(*BILL watches the DUCHESS with ever growing amazement as she sweeps about the stage being an imaginary hostess at an imaginary party.*)

DUCHESS. Lady Camberley! How are you? May I present Lord Edenbridge? Cynthia, my dear, you're looking lovelier than ever. And what a charming dress. Ah, there's Harry.
BILL. (*Joining in.*) Harry!
DUCHESS. Harry, I do declare you're putting on weight.
BILL. Oh, you little saucepot!
DUCHESS. How are you, Harry? Have a sherry? Sherry, dear? (*She holds out an imaginary glass. BILL dips in his finger.*)
BILL. Very dry sherry, Harry.
DUCHESS. Listen!
BILL. What?
DUCHESS. (*Dancing up center.*) The dance band is starting up.
BILL. (*Following her lead.*) Oh, thank God for that.
DUCHESS. It's playing my favorite waltz.
BILL. Oh, I love it! I love it!
DUCHESS. Now, you must dance like that graceful couple over there. (*She makes a sharp left turn as she dances downstage causing BILL to go flying down right.*) Oh, there's Lady Lind.

(*BILL dashes left to where the DUCHESS is pointing. He greets Lady Lind as if she were a foot tall.*)

BILL. Ah, Lady Lind! Hah-de-do?
DUCHESS. Go on, introduce her to someone. There's Lord Sheringham over there. Call him over.

(*BILL whistles shrilly.*)

DUCHESS. No, no, no!

BILL. (*To Lady Lind.*) No, no, no! Lady Lind, excuse me. (*He takes her imaginary hand and escorts her stage right.*) May I present Lord Sheringham. (*He looks up as though Lord Sheringham is towering over them.*) Lord Sheringham, this is Amarylla Lind. Amarylla! Keep you knickers on! For God's sake woman, you promised! (*BILL traps Lady Lind under his bowler. She is too fast for him. The bowler begins to move about the stage with BILL in pursuit.*)

DUCHESS. That'll do, William!

BILL. (*More antics.*) Amarylla, leave the bishop alone. Have you met my fiancee, Sally Smith? Isn't she a topper?

DUCHESS. William! Sally, of course, will not be invited to this party. It is vital that you make a good impression.

BILL. (*Crossing center to DUCHESS.*) Narc it, 'course she's coming.

DUCHESS. Can't you see that the more you progress, the more inappropriate Sally becomes. She understands that; why can't you?

BILL. What have you been saying to her?

DUCHESS. Never mind. Suffice it to say she knows what is best for you.

BILL. Whatever you do to me you'll never part me from my Sally.

DUCHESS. (*Crossing right to exit.*) We'll see about that in due course.

BILL. (*Pointing to her feet.*) Auntie, mind Lady Lind!

DUCHESS. Oh, I do beg your pardon!

[MUSIC CUE #9:UNDERSCORE]

(ELEC CUE: 28)
(CREW CUE: 8)
(CREW CUE: 9)

(*The DUCHESS stops to avoid Lady Lind. Then, realizing she has been duped, stomps off. BILL laughs, then crosses down left where HETHERSETT enters with BILL's mac. The scene changes to the Hareford Arms as BILL attempts to slip into the mac. Eventually, HETHERSETT ends up wearing the mac. A FOOTMAN presents BILL with rifle and hunting hat, and that is how he is seen entering the pub.)*

Scene 4

The Hareford Arms.

We are in the snug bar, where SALLY and ASSORTED LOCALS are enjoying a brew as a PIANIST gently plays his piano, right center. A BARMAN serves two LOCALS seated on a bench, left.

BILL enters, left, with pointed rifle. Much commotion. Finally BILL lowers the gun and crosses, center to SALLY.

(ELEC CUE: 29)

BILL. (*Calling from left.*) Sally!

SALLY. Bill!

BARMAN. (*Pointing to gun.*) My Lord!

BILL. (*Waving.*) Wotcher... I mean, I should bally dash it. Carry on, my good fellow.

SALLY. Coo, you don't half play the part, Bill.

BILL. (*Crossing to SALLY.*) It's easy when you get the hang of this. (*BILL waves at BENCH LOCALS. They wave back with drinks in hand, and spill drinks on themselves. They give BILL a dirty look. BILL moves down stage with SALLY.*) 'Ere, Sally, what do you think! There's gonna be a party at the 'all for me.

SALLY. (*Listlessly.*) That's nice.

(*SIR JOHN enters, right, unseen by BILL and SALLY.*)

BILL. To meet all the local nibs. It'll be a lark, don't you reckon?

SALLY. Well, I'm not coming. I'll only make you look stupid. Anyway, I've not been invited.

BILL. 'Course you're comin'. I'm inviting you.

SALLY. No, Bill. I've decided. I'm going back to Lambeth. Every day you grow more and more like a gentleman and I get more out of place.

BILL. You sound like my bleedin' aunt. You don't love me anymore, is that it? If you go back to Lambeth, I'll only follow you.

SALLY. No, Bill...

BILL. No!

(The vehemence of BILL's reply stops the PIANO PLAYER, and brings an embarrassed hush to the room)

BILL. You're staying here, and that's a bally fact. (*In the excitement, BILL has tucked the shotgun under this arm, with both barrels aiming at a couple of LOCALS. They raise their hands in horror. BILL clocks it and, looking for something to do with the gun, sticks it down his trousers as he exits. left.*)

SIR JOHN. (*Approaching SALLY.*) Can I get you another drink, Miss Smith?

SALLY. No thanks. Oh, it's Sir John, innit?

SIR JOHN. I knew the Duchess was ruining the peace of the Hall, but I had no idea she was ruining your life as well. It's more vital than ever that we persuade the Duchess to let him go back to Lambeth.

SALLY. He could never go back there now. He's started to like it here.

SIR JOHN. But he can't stay. He's an embarrassment to the whole family.

SALLY. His real roots are here, not in Lambeth. If I leave he'll settle down.

SIR JOHN. He'll only follow you. You heard him.

SALLY. Not if I can think of some way to show him that we are worlds apart. I've got to break it off.

ME AND MY GIRL

SIR JOHN. You're very fond of him, aren't you?

(During the following, LOCALS, and then SIR JOHN drift off, leaving SALLY and PIANO PLAYER alone.)

(ELEC CUE: 30)

[MUSIC CUE #10: ONCE YOU LOSE YOUR HEART]

SALLY.
ONCE YOU LOSE YOUR HEART, ONCE SOMEBODY TAKES IT
FROM THE PLACE IT RESTED IN BEFORE
ONCE YOU LOSE YOUR HEART, ONCE SOMEBODY WAKES IT
THEN IT ISN'T YOUR HEART ANYMORE

IT'S GONE BEFORE YOU KNEW IT COULD EVER GO THAT WAY
AND NOW YOU MUST PURSUE IT -- FOREVER AND A DAY

ONCE YOU LOSE YOUR HEART, ONCE SOMEBODY TAKES IT
THERE'S ONE THING CERTAIN FROM THE START
YOU'LL FIND FOREVER
YOU'VE GOT TO FOLLOW YOUR HEART

THEY SAY A GIRL SHOULD NEVER BE WITHOUT LOVE
AND ALL THE JOY THAT LOVE ALONE CAN BRING
ALL THAT I HAVE EVER LEARNT ABOUT LOVE
TELLS ME IT'S A VERY FUNNY THING

FOR WHEN YOUR HEART IS FANCY FREE
YOU HOPE SOME MAN WILL CHOOSE IT
BUT OH THE SPIN YOU FIND YOU'RE IN
THE VERY MOMENT THAT YOU LOSE IT

ONCE YOU LOSE YOUR HEART, ONCE SOMEBODY
  TAKES IT
FROM THE PLACE IT RESTED IN BEFORE
ONCE YOU LOSE YOUR HEART, ONCE SOMEBODY
  WAKES IT
THEN IT ISN'T YOUR HEART ANYMORE

IT'S GONE BEFORE YOU KNEW IT COULD EVER GO
  THAT WAY
AND NOW YOU MUST PURSUE IT FOREVER AND A
  DAY

ONCE YOU LOSE YOUR HEART, ONCE SOMEBODY
  TAKES IT
THERE'S ONE THING CERTAIN FROM THE START
YOU'VE GOT TO FOLLOW
YOU'VE GO TO FOLLOW YOUR HEART

(Lights fade out.) (ELEC CUE: 31)
(CREW CUE: 10)

Scene 5

Hareford Hall, exterior. The Terrace, early evening.

[MUSIC CUE #10A: PREPARATION FUGUE]

(The major elements are: the DUCHESS at her window, dressing, talking to SIR JOHN; JAQUIE at her window, dressing talking to GERALD; LADY BATTERSBY at her window, dressing talking to LORD BATTERSBY. The STAFF, at the bar and laying the table on the terrace, PARCHESTER and SOME GUESTS, waiting for PARTY GUESTS and BILL to arrive.)

(ELEC CUE: 32)

SIR JOHN. Maria, I want to talk.
DUCHESS. I'm busy.
SIR JOHN. I want to talk.
DUCHESS. The party.
GERALD. Jaquie, I want a word.
JAQUIE. Don't bother me.
GERALD. Must have a word.
JAQUIE. The party! (ELEC CUE: 33)
LADY BATTERSBY. Lord Lincoln is coming.
LORD BATTERSBY. Lord Wilmont is coming.
BARMAN #1. Orange and lemon and a twist of lime
BARMAN #2. Orange and lemon and a piece of lime.
BARMAN #1. Orange and lemon and a twist of lime.
BARMANS #2. Twist of lime, twist of lime.
SIR JOHN. A waste of time. A waste of time.
DUCHESS. I have to dress. I have to dress.
SIR JOHN. You're cruel to Sally and Bill, cruel.
DUCHESS. I have to dress.
SIR JOHN. Cruel to them, cruel.
DUCHESS. Have to dress.
GERALD. You're cruel to me, Jaquie, cruel.
JAQUIE. Where's my fan? Where's my fan?
GERALD. We're made for each other.
SIR JOHN. Bill and Sally are...
SIR JOHN, GERALD. ...made for each other.
SIR JOHN. Let Bill go!
HETHERSETT, WAITERS. Canapes, plates, trays.
BARMEN. Whiskey, gin and ice.

(A gong sounds.)

GUESTS, STAFF. They're late.
GERALD. He'll disgrace us. He'll shame us.
JAQUIE. He'll behave. Mummy's always right.
LORD BATTERSBY. A drink I think. I think a little drink.

ME AND MY GIRL

LADY BATTERSBY. Oh, no you don't, Freddy. Oh, no you don't.
LORD BATTERSBY. You're cruel to me, Clara, cruel to me.
GERALD. He'll say something frightful.
JAQUIE. He won't.
SIR JOHN. He'll say something rude.
DUCHESS. He daren't.
SIR JOHN. He's Cockney.
DUCHESS. He's Hareford. (ELEC CUE: 34)

(The FAMILY exit their windows and proceed to enter the terrace area.)

GUESTS, STAFF. Lovely evening, lovely evening.
ALL. They're late.
FOOTMAN. *(Announcing.)* Lady Damming.
LADY DAMMING. *(Entering upstage.)* How do you do?
FOOTMAN. Lord Wilmot, Lord French, and the Honourable May Miles.
WILMOT, FRENCH, MILES. *(Entering.)* Where is the earl? When can we meet him?
GUESTS. *(Vamp under the following.)* He's coming, he's coming.
OTHERS. *(Vamp under the following.)* He's coming, he's ready. He's coming, he's ready.

(DUCHESS enters up left followed by SIR JOHN, JAQUIE and GERALD. DUCHESS and SIR JOHN cross down center. JAQUIE and GERALD proceed down Left. The BATTERSBYS enter up right and proceed down right.)

SIR JOHN. He'll make us look fools.
DUCHESS. You already look a fool.
SIR JOHN. He'll make the family look ridiculous.
DUCHESS. He's been schooled.

JAQUIE. He'll cope.
GERALD. This is frightening.
LADY BATTERSBY. If he calls down for a pint of beer, I shall scream.
PARCHESTER. We musn't lose hope.
SIR JOHN. Have you re-orchestrated his table manners, taught him not to whistle, shown him...

(BILL enters up center. The vamp stops. BILL enters in silence.)

FOOTMAN. The Earl of Hareford.

(ELEC CUE: 35)

BILL. Ah, Aunt Maria. Gosh, you look abso-bally-lutely ravishing. Welcome to Hareford Hall, everyone, dash it.
SIR JASPER. Who's that?

[MUSIC CUE #10B: COCKTAIL MUSIC]

DUCHESS. *(As BILL crosses downstage.)* William.
JAQUIE. William!
GERALD. Good gad.
DUCHESS. William, may I present a very dear friend of mine? This is Celia Worthington-Worthington.
BILL. *(Taking her hand.)* Ah, Mrs. Worthington-Worthington. Delighted, delighted. Have you had a sherry, sherry? Gosh, I do declare, you've put on weight.
MRS. WORTHINGTON-WORTHINGTON. I beg your pardon?
DUCHESS. William is so original. *(The DUCHESS stamps BILL's foot as she escorts Mrs. WORTHINGTON-WORTHINGTON away. LADY DISS sees an opportunity and descends to BILL's right. MAY MILES to his left.)*
LADY DISS. Ah. Lord Hareford, I've been dying to meet you.

BILL. How too shatteringly interesting.
LADY DISS. Do you know my daughter, May.
BILL. Really? Thanks for the tip. (*BILL begins to kiss MAY's arm. LADY DISS moves between them.*)
LADY DISS. Are you enjoying your new life here?
BILL. Oh frightfully. Abso-bally-lutely yes. (*BILL pinches LADY DISS. She shrieks and leads MAY away, left. The BRIGHTONS enter up center.*)
FOOTMAN. The Earl and Countess...
BILL. You're late! (*Composing himself.*) Blood will flow. Have you had a channel ferry?

(*BILL and PARCHESTER circle DRINKS WAITER. LADY BRIGHTON mistakes BILL for PARCHESTER, and he plays along.*)

DUCHESS. (*Introducing PARCHESTER.*) Sophia, my dear. You know Mr. Parchester.
GENTLEMEN. (*Calling DUCHESS away.*) Your Grace...
LADY BRIGHTON. How do you do, Mr. Parchester. I'm Lady Brighton.
BILL. Ah, I love your beach.
LADY BRIGHTON. (*Taking BILL's drink.*) Now, tell me, which one is Lord Hareford. I gather he's a complete outsider. (*They cross downstage.*)
BILL. And so he bally is. A bally, bally, outsider.
LADY BRIGHTON. It's the Duchess I feel sorry for. (*She turns to survey the room. BILL dips his finger in the sherry glass and licks it. He produces a straw and proceeds to drain the glass.*)
BILL. The fellow's a sow's ear. Hoi polloi. Never been pukka, never.

(*Horrified, PARCHESTER takes the straw away from BILL who proceeds to eat the grapes from LADY BRIGHTON's hat. She turns back, almost catching BILL's actions.*)

LADY BRIGHTON. Maria means to part him from some frightful Brixton girl.
BILL. Oi! Lambeth, do you mind.
LADY BRIGHTON. I beg your pardon? (*Finds her glass empty. She looks at BILL. The both look at PARCHESTER who is holding the straw. BILL crosses away, up left.*) Which is Lord Hareford?
PARCHESTER. That was Lord Hareford.
FOOTMAN. Miss Sally Smith. (*SALLY enters in complete Cockney outfit from up center. PARCHESTER crosses right, LADY BRIGHTON crosses left. GUESTS gasp.*)
SALLY. Wotcher cocks! Hiya Lord 'areford. Seein as 'ow you invited me, I thought I'd come, and I've brought some of our royalty along with me. (*SALLY steps aside and the PEARLY KING and QUEEN enter.*) This is the Pearly King and Queen of Lambeth. And I've brought some of your' old mates along an' all. Knowin' as 'ow you'd be pleased to see them.

(*BILL stands gaping as a troupe of gaily-clad COCKNEYS enter. Chaos. FAMILY, GUESTS, and STAFF run for the stairs. COCKNEYS make themselves to home. BILL confronts SALLY.*)

BILL. Sally, what's this about?
SALLY. Well, you see, my Lord. You wanted me to come, but now, perhaps, you can see that me and my friends just don't fit in, so now I'm going back to Lambeth where I belong.

(*EVERYONE commenting at once.*)

BILL. Oi! Do you mind! You're talking to my girl, Sally. She done all this to prove that she don't belong. Well, all she's done is prove that I don't belong. I'm chucking this.

ME AND MY GIRL

DUCHESS. (*Right center.*) William!

BILL. (*Crossing to her.*) It's no good, auntie. I shall retire. On the annuity.

SALLY. No, Bill. I didn't do it for this.

BILL. Sally, East End is East End, and West End is West End. I'm off. (*He removes his jacket and throws it to a WAITER.*)

DUCHESS. (*Crossing right of BILL.*) Do you think I'll be beaten like this? You can't leave in the middle of a party. At least stay for dinner.

BILL. Only if my mates can stay.

DUCHESS. Oh, very well.

BILL. What about it, mates? You want to stay? (*The COCKNEYS agree. Much commotion.*)

BILL. But after dinner I'm going.

DUCHESS. We'll see about that.

BILL. You don't understand, do you? You could no more walk the Lambeth way than we could walk the Mayfair way.

(*During the following, BILL, SALLY and the COCKNEYS teach the FAMILY and GUESTS the Lambeth Walk. With seeming friendship and understanding all join in. The scene ends with EVERYONE going in to dinner.*)

[MUSIC CUE#11: THE LAMBETH WALK]

BILL.
LAMBETH -- YOU'VE NEVER SEEN
THE SKIES AIN'T BLUE, THE GRASS AIN'T GREEN
IT HASN'T GOT THE MAYFAIR TOUCH
BUT THAT DON'T MATTER VERY MUCH
WE PLAY A DIFFERENT WAY
NOT LIKE YOU, BUT A BIT MORE GAY
AND WHEN WE HAVE A BIT OF FUN -- OH BOY!

ANY TIME YOU'RE LAMBETH WAY

ANY EVENING -- ANY DAY
YOU'LL FIND US ALL
DOING THE LAMBETH WALK

EVERY LITTLE LAMBETH GAL
WITH HER LITTLE LAMBETH PAL
YOU'LL FIND US ALL
DOING THE LAMBETH WALK

EVERYTHING FREE AND EASY
DO AS YOU DARN WELL PLEASEY
WHY DON'T YOU MAKE YOUR WAY THERE?
GO THERE -- STAY THERE

ONCE YOU GET DOWN LAMBETH WAY
EVERY EVENING -- EVERY DAY
YOU'LL FIND YOURSELF
DOING THE LAMBETH WALK -- OI!
    SALLY.
ANY TIME YOU'RE LAMBETH WAY
ANY EVENING -- ANY DAY
YOU'LL FIND US ALL
DOING THE LAMBETH WALK -- OI!

EVERY LITTLE LAMBETH GAL
WITH HER LITTLE LAMBETH PAL
YOU'LL FIND 'EM ALL
DOING THE LAMBETH WALK
    BILL, SALLY & COCKNEYS.
EVERYTHING BRIGHT AND BREEZY
DO AS YOU DARN WELL PLEASEY
WHY DON'T YOU MAKE YOUR WAY THERE?
GO THERE -- STAY THERE

ONCE YOU GET DOWN LAMBETH WAY
EVERY EVENING -- EVERY DAY
YOU'LL FIND YOURSELF
DOING THE LAMBETH WALK -- OI!

BILL, SALLY, COCKNEYS & STAFF.
ANY TIME YOU'RE LAMBETH WAY
ANY EVENING -- ANY DAY
YOU'LL FIND US ALL
DOING THE LAMBETH WALK -- OI!

EVERY LITTLE LAMBETH GAL
WITH HER LITTLE LAMBETH PAL
YOU'LL FIND 'EM ALL
DOING THE LAMBETH WALK -- OI!

(ELEC CUE: 38)

(*During the next musical bridge the COCKNEYS play a "spoons" accompaniment.*)

BILL, SALLY, COCKNEYS & STAFF.
DOING THE LAMBETH WALK -- OI!
GUESTS. (*As musically dictated.*)
ANY TIME YOU'RE LAMBETH WAY
ANY EVENING -- ANY DAY
YOU'LL FIND US ALL
DOING THE LAMBETH WALK

EVERY LITTLE LAMBETH GAL
WITH HER LITTLE LAMBETH PAL
YOU'LL FIND 'EM ALL
DOING THE LAMBETH WALK -- OI!
ALL. (*But FAMILY GROUP.*)
EVERYTHING FREE AND EASY
DO AS YOU DARN WELL PLEASEY
WHY DON'T YOU MAKE YOUR WAY THERE?

FAMILY GROUP.
GO THERE --
ALL.
STAY THERE
FULL COMPANY.
ONCE YOU GET DOWN LAMBETH WAY
EVERY EVENING -- EVERY DAY

YOU'LL FIND YOURSELF
DOING THE LAMBETH WALK -- OI!

ANY TIME YOU'RE LAMBETH WAY
ANY EVENING -- ANY DAY
YOU'LL FIND US ALL
DOING THE LAMBETH WALK

EVERY LITTLE LAMBETH GAL
WITH HER LITTLE LAMBETH PAL
YOU'LL FIND 'EM ALL
DOING THE LAMBETH WALK -- OI!

EVERYTHING FREE AND EASY
DO AS YOU DARN WELL PLEASEY
WHY DON'T YOU MAKE YOUR WAY THERE?
GO THERE -- STAY THERE

ONCE YOU GET DOWN LAMBETH WAY
EVERY EVENING -- EVERY DAY
YOU'LL FIND YOURSELF
DOING THE LAMBETH WALK -- OI!

ANY TIME YOU'RE LAMBETH WAY
ANY EVENING -- ANY DAY
YOU'LL FIND US ALL
DOING THE LAMBETH WALK -- OI!
EVERYTHING FREE AND EASY
DO AS YOU DARN WELL PLEASEY
WHY DON'T YOU MAKE YOUR WAY THERE?
GO THERE -- STAY THERE

ONCE YOU GET DOWN LAMBETH WAY
EVERY EVENING -- EVERY DAY
YOU'LL FIND YOURSELF
DOING THE LAMBETH WALK -- OI!

ANY TIME YOU'RE LAMBETH WAY

ANY EVENING -- ANY DAY
YOU'LL FIND US ALL
DOING THE LAMBETH --
DOING THE LAMBETH WALK -- OI!

(*Dinner gong.*)

    HETHERSETT. Your Grace, dinner is served.

    [MUSIC CUE #11A: LAMBETH PLAYOFF]

  ALL.
ANY TIME YOU'RE LAMBETH WAY
ANY EVENING -- ANY DAY
YOU'LL FIND US ALL
DOING THE LAMBETH WALK

(ELEC CUE: 39)

EVERY LITTLE LAMBETH GAL
WITH HER LITTLE LAMBETH PAL
YOU'LL FIND 'EM ALL
DOING THE LAMBETH WALK -- OI!

EVERYTHING FREE AND EASY
DO AS YOU DARN WELL PLEASEY
WHY DON'T YOU MAKE YOUR WAY THERE?
    DUCHESS & COMPANY.
GO THERE --
    BILL & COMPANY.
STAY THERE
    ALL.
ONCE YOU GET DOWN LAMBETH WAY
EVERY EVENING -- EVERY DAY
YOU'LL FIND YOURSELF
DOING THE LAMBETH
DOING THE LAMBETH WALK -- OI!

(ELEC CUE: 40)
(CREW CUE: 11)

CURTAIN

[MUSIC CUE #12: ENTR'ACTE]

ACT II

Scene 1

The garden of Hareford Hall.
Upstage we can see the facade of the Hall. The large part of the stage is taken up with lawn, shrubs and trees.
The curtain rises on a freeze of GUESTS, some dressed casually, some in tennis clothes, and SERVANTS. The FAMILY is represented by LORD and LADY BATTERSBY, SIR JASPER TRING, JAQUIE and GERALD. PARCHESTER is also in attendance.

[MUSIC CUE #13: THE SUN HAS GOT HIS HAT ON]

ALL.
THE SUN HAS GOT HIS HAT ON
HIP HIP HIP HOORAY
THE SUN HAS GOT HIS HAT ON
AND HE'S COMING OUT TODAY

NOW WE'LL ALL BE HAPPY
HIP HIP HIP HOORAY
THE SUN HAS GOT HIS HAT ON
AND HE'S COMING OUT TODAY
    GERALD.
HE'S BEEN ROASTING PEANUTS
OUT IN TIMBUCTU
NOW HE'S COMING BACK
TO DO THE SAME FOR YOU
    ALL.
SO JUMP INTO YOUR SUNBATH
HIP HIP HIP HOORAY
THE SUN HAS GOT HIS HAT ON

AND HE'S COMING OUT TODAY

    GERALD.
JOY BELLS ARE RINGING
THE SONG BIRDS ARE SINGING
AND EVERYONE'S HAPPY AND GAY
DULL DAYS ARE OVER
WE'LL SOON BE IN CLOVER
SO PACK ALL YOUR TROUBLES AWAY

THE SUN HAS GOT HIS HAT ON
HIP HIP HIP HOORAY
THE SUN HAS GOT HIS HAT ON
AND HE'S COMING OUT TODAY
    ALL.
NOW WE'LL ALL BE HAPPY
HIP HIP HIP HOORAY
THE SUN HAS GOT HIS HAT ON
AND HE'S COMING OUT TODAY
    GERALD.
ALL THE LITTLE BOYS EXCITED
ALL THE LITTLE GIRLS DELIGHTED
WHAT A LOT OF FUN FOR EVERYONE
SITTING IN THE SUN ALL DAY

(*GERALD scat sings the next verse.*)

    ALL.
SO JUMP INTO YOUR SUNBATH
HIP HIP HIP HOORAY
THE SUN HAS GOT HIS HAT ON
AND HE'S COMING OUT TODAY

(*Tap break.*)　　　　　　　　　　(ELEC CUE: 42)
　　　　　　　　　　　　　　　　(ELEC CUE: 43)
    ALL.
SO JUMP INTO YOUR SUNBATH
HIP HIP HIP HOORAY

THE SUN HAS GOT HIS HAT ON
AND HE'S COMING OUT
HE'S COMING OUT
THE SUN HAS GOT HIS HAT ON
AND HE'S COMING OUT TODAY

(ELEC CUE: 44)

(JAQUIE and GERALD are playing croquet as GUESTS, STAFF, and FAMILY with the exception of SIR JAPSER, exit slowly. PARCHESTER is eating a bit of cake from a plate at the right garden table. JAQUIE is down left, center. She sets her shot.)

JAQUIE. Gerald, have you seen William at all today?

GERALD. *(Center.)* No.

JAQUIE. Did those frightful Cockney people go home last night?

GERALD. The Duchess packed them all off at about half past two in the morning.

JAQUIE. But William stayed?

GERALD. And Sally.

JAQUIE. Sally! How dare she? She's trying to get William to run away with her.

GERALD. *(Crossing to JAQUIE.)* Eh? I thought she wanted him to stay here.

JAQUIE. *(Crossing away, center.)* Oh, Gerald you really don't know anything about women.

GERALD. I may not know anything about women, but dash it, Jaquie, I like you.

JAQUIE. She's clever, very clever. She knows if she plays the little martyr William will want her all the more.

(MAID enters right with cup of coffee and crosses to PARCHESTER. JAQUIE crosses back to her shot, left. GERALD is standing in the way.)

JAQUIE. Gerald, do you mind.
GERALD. (*Steps out of the way.*) Oh.
JAQUIE. (*Striking the ball, left.*) Mummy must get rid of her. (*Bad shot.*) Damn!
GERALD. I say, good shot.

(*JAQUIE exits left. PARCHESTER calls GERALD. SALLY wanders in up center through the garden gate.*)

PARCHESTER. (*Presenting coffee.*) Gerald, come have a cup of Rosie Lee.
GERALD. Thank you. Ugh! This is coffee!
PARCHESTER. That's right, coffee, yes.
GERALD. But I thought that Rosie Lee was rhyming slang for cup of tea.
PARCHESTER. Ah, but this is blank rhyming slang.
GERALD. Blank rhyming slang?
PARCHESTER. Well, modern poets these days write in blank verse. Verse that doesn't rhyme. This is blank rhyming slang. Cain and Abel; chair, that sort of thing. (*Crosses right to the table. Cake plate down. MAID exits with coffee. GERALD, alone, addresses SALLY as he exits, left.*)
GERALD. Mad. He's turning the whole world stark staring mad. The sooner he bally goes, the bally better!

(*DUCHESS and SIR JOHN enter down left. She with mallet and ball; he with whiskey flask. She motions SALLY downstage. PARCHESTER and HETHERSETT stand upstage of them.*)

DUCHESS. Thank you for coming out, Sally, I wanted to speak to you before you return to London. You know it's quite impossible for William to go back to Lambeth with you.
SALLY. 'Course I do. What d'you think I was trying to show him last night?

SIR JOHN. Maria, you can't still mean to ...

DUCHESS. Hush, you futile man. (*DUCHESS hands her croquet and ball to PARCHESTER and crosses down center, motioning SALLY to follow.*) I appreciated what you tried to do, unfortunately, it had the opposite effect. Therefore, you must go to Bill...

SIR JOHN. Maria, it crossed my mind...

DUCHESS. Not a long journey. You must speak to Bill and break it off. Finally, once and for all. Tell him you no longer love him. (*DUCHESS turns away from SALLY and indicates for PARCHESTER to set her ball. He does so, and hands her the mallet.*)

SALLY. But even if I leave he'll only follow me. You heard what he said.

DUCHESS. (*Turning back.*) Oh, I think you could stop him following you, Sally, if you really wanted to. If not...

SALLY. Yes, I know. Well, I won't spoil his chances. He means too much to me for that. Leave it to me.

DUCHESS. (*Turning away.*) You'll find him in the library.

SALLY. What's he doing there?

DUCHESS. I have persuaded him that he must at least make his maiden speech in the House of Lords.

PARCHESTER. (*Crossing to SALLY's left.*) As a peer of the realm, he has to appear there in the robes and coronet of an earl and make a maiden speech.

SALLY. Blimey, whatever is he going to speak on?

PARCHESTER. The Public Right of Way Bill of 1824. (*PARCHESTER returns upstage of the DUCHESS. She turns back to SALLY.*)

DUCHESS. After you have seen him I will give orders for a car to take you away to Lambeth. (*She motions to HETHERSETT who crosses to SALLY, takes her suitcase and exits up right.*) You must make sure that he has no intention of following you.

SIR JOHN. You're a wicked interfering old bat.

DUCHESS. I'm impervious to flattery. (*She hits ball and exits left followed by PARCHESTER.*) Come Parchester.
SIR JOHN. You can't let her do this to you.
SALLY. But she's right. Bill belongs here I don't.
SIR JOHN. You must stand up to her. Show her who's boss.
SALLY. She already knows who's boss. She is.
SIR JOHN. Leave it to me. (*DUCHESS enters down left in search of SIR JOHN.*) I'll tell the old witch -- (*Sees her.*) -- witch, which reminds me; it's my shot I think.

[MUSIC CUE #14: TAKE IT ON THE CHIN]

(*SIR JOHN follows the DUCHESS out left. SALLY starts to follow, thinks better of it, then begins to weep, softly. SIR JASPER, who has been watching from upstage, crosses to her.*)

SIR JASPER. Are you all right? Are you crying?
SALLY. No, I'm okay. People often look like they're crying when really they're sort of laughing.
SIR JASPER. Eh?
SALLY. I'm laughing.
SIR JASPER. What?
SALLY. I'm laughing. (ELEC CUE: 45)
ONCE MY FATHER SAID, AND MY MOTHER SAID
AND MY SISTER SAID, AND MY BROTHER SAID
NOW YOU'RE GROWING UP SOON YOU'RE GOING
   TO FALL OUT
OF THE FAMILY ROUNDABOUT

THEN MY FATHER SAID, AND MY MOTHER SAID
AND MY SISTER SAID, AND MY BROTHER SAID
THERE'S ONE LITTLE THING YOU SHOULD
   CERTAINLY KNOW
WHEN INTO THE WORLD YOU GO

ME AND MY GIRL

TAKE YOUR TROUBLES ON THE CHIN
AND THOUGH YOU GET AN EARFUL
DON'T DESPAIR OR TEAR YOUR HAIR
FOR HEAVEN'S SAKE KEEP CHEERFUL

THAT'S WHAT FATHER SAID, THAT'S WHAT MOTHER SAID
THAT'S WHAT SISTER SAID, THAT'S WHAT BROTHER SAID
THEY WERE CERTAINLY RIGHT IN TELLING ME SO
AND I THINK THAT YOU SHOULD KNOW

HERE'S A LITTLE TRICK
WHENEVER THINGS GET A LITTLE BIT THICK
JUST YOU TAKE IT ON THE CHIN
TURN ON A LITTLE GRIN
AND SMILE, SMILE

HERE'S A LITTLE RUSE
TO COUNTERACT AN ATTACK OF THE BLUES
JUST YOU TAKE IT ON THE CHIN
TURN ON A LITTLE GRIN
AND SMILE

WHAT'S THE USE OF WORRYING
'BOUT A SINGLE BLESSED THING
AFTER ALL IS DONE AND SAID
PRETTY SOON WE'LL ALL BE DEAD

SO AS WE'RE ALIVE
IF THERE'S A BOTHER YOU WANT TO SURVIVE
JUST YOU TAKE IT ON THE CHIN
CULTIVATE A LITTLE GRIN
AND SMILE
    SIR JASPER. Eh?
    SALLY.
HERE'S A LITTLE TRICK

WHENEVER THINGS GET A LITTLE BIT THICK
JUST YOU TAKE IT ON THE CHIN
TURN ON A LITTLE GRIN
AND SMILE

WHAT'S THE USE OF WORRYING
'BOUT A SINGLE BLESSED THING
AFTER ALL IS DONE AND SAID
PRETTY SOON WE'LL ALL BE DEAD

SO AS WE'RE ALIVE
IF THERE'S A BOTHER YOU WANT TO SURVIVE
JUST YOU TAKE IT ON THE CHIN
CULTIVATE A LITTLE GRIN
JUST YOU TAKE IT ON THE CHIN
CULTIVATE A LITTLE GRIN
AND SMILE, SMILE, SMILE (ELEC CUE: 46)
(CREW CUE: 12)

(The scene fades to black.)

[MUSIC CUE #14A: SCENE CHANGE]

Scene 2

The library.

The library shelves range across the stage, containing many and varied volumes. Above the shelves are hung the ancestors' portraits. To each side of the stage there stands another bookcase with a classical bust resting on top.

The room is furnished with a small drinks table, down left and a small round table down right with ancient tombs of all sizes. The mobile library steps stand by the upstage shelves, and a tiger-skin rug is spread on the floor down center.

ME AND MY GIRL

Lights up to reveal BILL sitting at the table, almost swamped by a huge and ancient volume, which he is studying. He is dressed in full peer's regalia -- ermine trimmed robe and coronet. SALLY stands in front of drinks table.

(ELEC CUE: 47)

BILL. My lords and mistresses. Your lordships, your worships, your fish and chips, my noble lords, I rise to my feet on this suspicious occasion, and having risen to my feet...(*He steps forward, and we see that his cloak is trapped under the foot of the chair. He trips up, dropping the book, and sending the coronet flying.*)

SALLY. (*At his side.*) Bill! You all right!

BILL. No, I'm just doin' some press-ups.

SALLY. (*Handing coronet.*) And you've dropped your cornet.

BILL. That's a coronet. (*BILL takes the coronet, stands, and moves about, showing himself off. He sets the coronet on the round table, and rights the chair, center.*)

SALLY. You don't half look smart, Bill.

BILL. Do you reckon?

SALLY. Why is your get up all trimmed with vermin like that?

BILL. Vermin? This is ermine.

SALLY. (*Pointing at the black flecks in the ermine.*) Well those look like vermin.

BILL. Yeah, they do and all. (*He tries without success to brush them off.*)

SALLY. (*Opening book in front of her.*) What's this book then?

BILL. That is The History of The Harefords.

(*SALLY picks a cut-out tree from one of the pages.*)

BILL. Put that down, that's my family tree. It's got pictures of all my ancestors from 1066.

SALLY. Oh yeah, I learned all that when I was at school.

BILL. Then you know who invaded Britain in 1066.

SALLY. 'Course, the Romans.

BILL. No! The Romans come over in BBC. I'm talking about 1066 Anno Dominoes. The Battle of Hastings when 'Arold was 'it in the heye with a harrow.

SALLY. Oh yeah -- I remember now. He put an apple on his head and said, "Shoot, Father, I am not afraid."

BILL. (*Kneels by her side.*) No, Sally, you're thinking of George Washington and the cherry tree. (*He stands on his cloak and nearly strangles himself.*)

SALLY. No, George Washington sat under a cherry tree and discovered gravity.

BILL. (*Crosses right. The cloak is out of control.*) No, look, let's sort this out once and for all. (*He rolls up his cloak round his arms.*) We really started with King John. (*He crossed to SALLY and points to a page in the book.*) That geezer there was Simon de Hareford, who forced the King to sign the Magna Charta in 1215 and so founded a strong English constitution. Then he married the King's cousin and had fourteen sons.

SALLY. Blimey! He must 'ave 'ad a strong constitution.

BILL. And this is him again, forcing him to sign the actual parchment. (*Lets go of the book, and SALLY, unable to hold the weight of it on her own, falls to the floor. BILL walks proudly round, making his flowing cloak billow in the air, and then sits on the chair, so that the cloak forms a circle around him.*)

SALLY. Lummie, ain't you grand?

BILL .(*Stands on chair.*) Sal, see that geezer there? That's Richard Hareford otherwise known as Tricky Dickie. (*He falls off the chair and gets caught up in the cape.*) He's the one wha actually fought Joan of Arc. (*Crosses to library steps.*)

SALLY. (*Following.*) Joan of Arc, but your ancestors don't go back that far.

BILL. What chew talking about. She come after King John, you're getting your history all muddled. (*Climbs the library ladder. SALLY follows.*)

SALLY. Oh no I'm not. Everyone knows Joan of Arc was married to Noah.

BILL. Not *that* ark. I'm talking about the French 'erk' Joan of Arc, you nerk! She was a beautiful maiden who rode against the English with nothing but her courage. (*As BILL walks away from the steps, SALLY who has held onto his cloak is pulled along.*)

SALLY. Oh, yeah, she rode her lily white horse through the streets of Covent Garden.

BILL. Sally, that was Florence Nightingale! ([MUSIC CUE #15: BRITISH GRENADIERS (SECOND START)] *He sweeps round again but this time misses the chair and ends up on the floor.*)

SALLY. Oh, Bill! Whoo! Who's that geezer?

BILL. That's Jonathan Hareford, the mad sea dog.

SALLY. Sea dog?

BILL. Explorer. He discovered New Jersey. Do you realize that Jonathan actually saw Sir Walter Raleigh spread out his cloak.

SALLY. (*Climbing off the ladder.*) Spread out his cloak? Whatever for?

BILL. Sally, don't you remember who passed over?

SALLY. Oh, yeah, the Israelites.

BILL. (*Crosses to her.*) You are pretending to be more ignorant than what you actually are, aren't you?

SALLY. (*Crossing away, she moves chair to table.*) What would I do that for?

BILL. (*Arms around her.*) You're trying to put me off -- like you tried last night at that party. But I'll tell you this, my girl, it ain't working. I'm gonna do this speech and then you and I are going to get married and live on the annuity.

SALLY. No, Bill, I've come to say goodbye.

BILL. Now don't start that all over again.

SALLY. Can't you see why the duchess has stuffed all these ancestors into your nut? To make you feel like a gentleman and me like a worm. She's making a gentleman of you, Bill.

BILL. She can't make a sow's purse out of a silk ear.

SALLY. She's already got you talking like the BBC.

BILL. (*Crossing left.*) Oh come on.

SALLY. And walking like Douglas Fairbanks.

BILL. Don't be so bally daft.

SALLY. You even swear all posh. You've got to marry someone with good blood.

BILL. Well, you're not anemic.

SALLY. It's not blue, though. Goodbye, Bill.

BILL. (*Rushing to her.*) Here, what's going on, girl? Oh, please, babe! Don't cry.

SALLY. (*Turning away.*) I'm not.

BILL. Well don't dribble down me vermin then. Oi! I'll clobber you with my ancestors. (*He raises book threateningly.*)

SALLY. It's no good, Bill.

BILL. (*Returning book to table.*) That does it! I'm not standing here watching you crying. I'm not having this. I'm going to sort it out with her once and for all.

SALLY. You'll never stand up to her, Bill.

BILL. (*Crosses to the drinks table and picks up the brandy decanter.*) Oh won't I? We'll see about that!

SALLY. Put that down.

BILL. (*Drinks from the decanter.*) I already have. Now I'm ready for her. (ELEC CUE: 48)

(*Swirls his cloak round in a dramatic gesture, enveloping JASPER, who has just entered. He then sweeps out, carrying JASPER with him.*)

[MUSIC CUE #16:ONCE YOU LOSE YOUR HEART (REPRISE)]

SALLY.
ONCE YOU LOSE YOUR HEART
ONCE SOMEBODY TAKES IT
FROM THE PLACE IT RESTED IN BEFORE
ONCE YOU LOSE YOUR HEART
ONCE SOMEBODY WAKES IT
THEN IT ISN'T YOUR HEART ANYMORE
IT'S GONE BEFORE YOU KNEW
IT COULD EVER GO THAT WAY
AND NOW YOU MUST PURSUE IT
FOREVER AND A DAY

ONCE YOU LOSE YOUR HEART
ONCE SOMEBODY TAKES IT
THERE'S ONE THING CERTAIN FROM THE START
YOU'VE GOT TO FOLLOW...

(HETHERSETT enters.)

HETHERSETT. The car is ready, Miss.
(ELEC CUE: 49)
(SALLY exits, followed the HETHERSETT. The DUCHESS enters right with BILL, who brandishes a rapier. Through the next speech BILL tries without success to get a word in edgeways.)

DUCHESS. Silence, silence. I will have silence. The idea is preposterous. It is absurd. You know it is absurd. Noblesse oblige. Sally does not arise -- she simply does not arise. Presently I shall force Sir John as the other trustee to agree -- God help me -- that you are a suitable person to stay here as Master of Hareford.

(BILL turns an imaginary crank in the DUCHESS's back as if winding her up.)

DUCHESS. Next, I shall marry you to Jaqueline...

(Emitting a cry of horror, BILL stabs himself under the arm with the rapier, and falls onto the tiger-skin rug.)

DUCHESS. ...she doesn't love you but she wants your title and money. Nothing wrong with that. Love. Love is for the middle classes.

BILL. Middle classes? What about the King? The King married for love.

DUCHESS. *(Crossing right.)* Middle class, middle class foreigners, that whole family -- Oh, if only I could say something. If I could find words to speak. But no, there you lie and chatter -- chatter -- chatter. Argue -- argue -- argue. While I can't get a word in edgeways.

BILL. *(Playing with tiger.)* So you won't talk, eh?

DUCHESS. William, read that motto. *(She points to a great shield of armorial bearings.)*

BILL. *(Reading.)* Nobbles oblige.

DUCHESS. Noblesse oblige. Do you know what that means?

BILL. No, and I don't want to.

(ELEC CUE: 50)

(Suddenly one of the ANCESTORS in the portrait comes to life. It is SIMON DE HAREFORD. Throughout this scene the DUCHESS does not at any time see the ANCESTORS. She is always Downstage of them. Only BILL can see them.)

(ELEC CUE: 51)

SIMON. Nobility has its obligations!

BILL. *(To tiger.)* Here, did you see that? *(Tiger flies offstage.* (CREW CUE: 13)

That was Simon de Hareford.

(Another ANCESTOR comes to life. It is THOMAS HAREFORD.) (ELEC CUE: 52)

THOMAS. There's a price to pay for land and titles.

ME AND MY GIRL

BILL. All right, calm down. What is occurring? That was Thomas Hareford. He burnt four hundred people in one day. (ELEC CUE:53)

THOMAS. Six hundred! At your service.

(Another ANCESTOR -- RICHARD HAREFORD -- comes to life.)
(ELEC CUE: 54)

RICHARD. Riches carry responsibility!

(Now all six of the portraits come to life.)

BILL. My ancestors! (ELEC CUE: 55)

[MUSIC CUE #17: SONG OF HAREFORD]

DUCHESS.
THE STORY OF HAREFORD -- HANDED DOWN
SINCE WILLIAM THE NORMAN WORE THE CROWN
THE STORY OF HAREFORD -- THROUGH THE AGES
TELLS OF HONOR AND GLORY ON ALL ITS PAGES
NOBLESSE OBLIGE (ELEC CUE: 56)
    ANCESTORS.
NOBLESSE OBLIGE
    DUCHESS.
NOBLESSE OBLIGE
    ANCESTORS.
NOBLESSE OBLIGE
    ALL.
NOBLESSE OBLIGE
    DUCHESS.
MEN OF HAREFORD -- THE AGES TELL
KNEW THEIR DUTY AND DID IT WELL
CHERISHED THE PROUD HAREFORD STORY
LIVED AND DIED STILL ADDING TO ITS GLORY

HAREFORD STANDS WHERE HAREFORD STOOD

THANKS TO MEN OF HAREFORD BLOOD
LET IT GO ON THAT WAY -- I PRAY THAT IT MAY --
(CREW CUE: 14)
(ELEC CUE: 57)
TO THE MEN OF HAREFORD OF TODAY

(PORTRAIT ANCESTORS' tap break.)

(ELEC CUE: 57a)
(CREW CUE: 15)
(ELEC CUE: 58)

(ANCESTORS enter through central library shelves. They provide a pageant of the Hareford line that stretches in costume from Norman to the twentieth century.)

ANCESTORS.
MEN OF HAREFORD -- THE AGES TELL
KNEW THEIR DUTY AND DID IT WELL
CHERISHED THE PROUD HAREFORD STORY
LIVED AND DIED STILL ADDING TO ITS GLORY

HAREFORD STANDS WHERE HAREFORD STOOD
THANKS TO MEN OF HAREFORD BLOOD
LET IT GO ON THAT WAY -- WE PRAY THAT IT MAY --
TO THE MEN OF HAREFORD OF TODAY
DUCHESS & ANCESTORS.
NOBLESSE OBLIGE/NOBLESSE OBLIGE/NOBLESSE OBLIGE

MEN OF HAREFORD -- THE AGES TELL
KNEW THEIR DUTY AND DID IT WELL
CHERISHED THE PROUD HAREFORD STORY
LIVED AND DIED STILL ADDING TO ITS GLORY

HAREFORD STANDS WHERE HAREFORD STOOD
THANKS TO MEN OF HAREFORD BLOOD
LET IT GO ON THAT WAY -- WE PRAY THAT IT MAY --
(ELEC CUE: 59)

TO THE MEN OF HAREFORD OF TODAY
(ELEC CUE: 60)

(Dance Reprise. ANCESTORS exit as they arrived. SIR JOHN followed by PARCHESTER and HETHERSETT pushing a tea trolley enter left.)
(ELEC CUE: 61)

DUCHESS. Here comes Sir John. He will tell you the meaning of Noblesse Oblige, if he's not too tight. (*Exits.*)

BILL. (*Manic.*) John, John you should have seen the pictures. All my ancestors, all dancing. There was Simon de Hareford giving it some of this, and Joan of Arc...There's been a right bloody royal knees up here. (*BILL points to the right bookcase bust. It's mouth moves. BILL and SIR JOHN are shocked.*)

SIR JOHN. My God, you must be as drunk as I am. It's the only way with Maria. She's like Mussolini, without the charm.

(BILL attempts to sit in the chair SALLY has placed at the right round table. At the same moment, SIR JOHN, unaware that there is no chair center, attempts to sit. PARCHESTER, saving SIR JOHN, grabs BILL's chair for SIR JOHN who promptly sits. BILL, unaware that his chair is gone, sits also. It is not until SIR JOHN stares at BILL that he realizes there is no chair beneath him, and falls to the floor. SIR JOHN sees HETHERSETT, left, and crosses to him.)

SIR JOHN. Thank you, Hethersett. (*Realizing it's tea.*) Tea! How dare you. I had an aunt once who drank tea. Dead before she saw fifty. Mind you the steam roller didn't help matters. Come on, my boy, let's get squiffy. (*SIR JOHN crosses up behind drinks table and pours for himself and BILL. BILL joins at JOHN's right. PARCHESTER is amusing himself with book titles during the following.*)

BILL. John, she's trying to turn me into a nobble.

SIR JOHN. A what?

BILL. A toffee-nosed herbert like you. No offense.

SIR JOHN. None taken, my dear fellow. Your very good health.

BILL. And so are you, John, so are you. (*They drink.*)

SIR JOHN. Extraordinary! As soon as I saw you, I said to myself, "Johnny," I always call myself "Johnny," you know. Well, that is my name you understand. "Johnny," I said, "this man you are looking at here is a snuttergipe." (*To BILL.*) I think you mean "guttersnipe." "This is a man I would walk a mile in tight shoes to avoid. This is nothing but an utter, unmitigated Yahoo!"

BILL. (*Almost in tears.*) That is the most beautiful thing anyone has ever said to me. (*Handing SIR JOHN his watch back.*) 'Ere you go, my son.

SIR JOHN. How do you do that?

BILL. (*Falling into chair by drink table.*) Let's have another drink, my old china.

SIR JOHN. Wotcha, me old cock!

(*BILL reaches for glass at drinks table, but his reach is too short. He looks at his arms, horrified, that one arm appears shorter than the other. During the following, he manages to pull one arm longer at the expense of the other, and get his drink. He drinks, then stands.*)

BILL. Don't let the old battle-axe hear you saying that, Squire. There won't half be a lot of trouble. If Sally catches me drinking this much, there ain't 'alf going to be a lot of trouble.

SIR JOHN. Bill, the duchess is the key. We've got to get the duchess to see Sally in her true light.

PARCHESTER. (*Suddenly between them.*) If I may suggest, Sir John...

SIR JOHN. Where the hell did he come from?

PARCHESTER. You must both stand up to her Grace. Tell her, if I may use the phrase, where to go.

SIR JOHN. With knobs on!
BILL. (*Arm around PARCHESTER's neck.*) You on our side, Cedric?
SIR JOHN. (*Arm around PARCHESTER's neck.*) Cedric? Is that your name? I never knew you had a name. My, what short arms you have Parchester? (*BILL and SIR JOHN operate arms as if they were PARCHESTER's. Glasses off, wipe glasses, blow nose, etc.*) Cedric, my boy, in this battle you are either with us or you're not with us.
BILL. It's all for one and one for all.
SIR JOHN. And I'm for another drink.
BILL. Yeah, me an 'all.
PARCHESTER. Well, then, I suppose I must be with you. We must present a united front.
BILL. So what d'yer advise then, Cedrico?

[MUSIC CUE #17A: THE FAMILY SOLICITOR (2nd REPRISE)]

PARCHESTER. Well -- (*Pulls flower from vase.*)
AS THE FAMILY SOLICITOR...
HERE'S MY ADVICE TO YOU, AS THE FAMILY...
DUCHESS. (*Entering up left to center.*) That'll do, Parchester. Pay close attention. I have at last succeeded in uniting the whole family behind me in this matter.

(*SIR JOHN and PARCHESTER slip quietly out, as the FAMILY, arguing, enters up right.*)

DUCHESS. We demand that you give up Sally at all costs.
BILL. You and the family demand! Well, let me tell you something. We...(*He turns to realize that SIR JOHN and PARCHESTER have evaporated.*) I demand that I marry Sally or die an old maid. (*To the portraits.*) Whatever they say ... 'ere, where've they gone?
DUCHESS. William, pull yourself together and come here.

BILL. I won't come here.

DUCHESS. (*Imperiously.*) Come here!

BILL. (*Crossing to left of DUCHESS.*) Shan't! I intend to be master of my own house.

DUCHESS. Listen to me.

BILL. No, you listen to me. You and the family can all go to blazes. And he told me to tell you so. (*He points to PARCHESTER who has surreptitiously reentered. Horrified, PARCHESTER hides behind the FAMILY group.*) And Sir John told me to tell you personally to all go to blazes, and then the fat will be in the fire. (*He crosses above round table, raises book over his head.*) The History of the Harefords starts with me! (*He throws the book to the floor.*) And this is what I think of past history!

DUCHESS. (*Crosses, right, to BILL.*) How dare you! This shows how much you need a proper wife to teach you how to behave. Sally is the last person for that position. The last. Finally and positively the last! (*Exits up right followed by the FAMILY. BILL staggers center shaking his fists at the departing group. SIR JOHN runs on from down left, crosses to BILL.*)

SIR JOHN. Bill! I've just seen Sally leaving in the car.

BILL. (*Sits in chair, defeated.*) It's her. She's made her go back to Lambeth.

SIR JOHN. I'll get Maria back -- I'll show her that it's wrong to part two lovers. I'll stand up to her. (*Falls down.*)

BILL. 'Ere, John, I want to tell you something. You know Sally -- she's my girl. I've never loved anyone else. Well, you know, (*Kissing SIR JOHN on the forehead.*) except you, of course.

SIR JOHN. Of course.

BILL. She's everything to me ...

SIR JOHN. Me too. She's a hard old battleship, but I love her.

BILL. (*Standing.*) What, Sally?

SIR JOHN. No, Maria.

ME AND MY GIRL

BILL. Johnny, why is everything spinning round? What have you been doing to this room, you little rascal?

SIR JOHN. (*Standing.*) Not me, old sport. Must be something to do with sun spots. What's making everything go round?

[MUSIC CUE #18 :LOVE MAKES THE WORLD GO ROUND]

    BILL. No, I know what it is.   (ELEC CUE: 62)
THE WORLD KEEPS ON TURNING
YOU CAN'T STOP IT TURNING
IT'S LOVE MAKES THE WORLD GO ROUND
    SIR JOHN.
AN OLD LOVE, A NEW LOVE
SO LONG AS IT'S TRUE LOVE
IT'S LOVE MAKES THE WORLD GO ROUND
    BILL.
WITHOUT LOVE NOBODY WOULD SING
    SIR JOHN.
WITHOUT LOVE NO WEDDING BELLS RING
    BOTH.
AND THOUGH PEOPLE DOUBT IT
THEY CAN'T LIVE WITHOUT IT
ALL OVER THE WORLD THEY'VE FOUND
THAT LOVE MAKES THE WORLD GO ROUND
    (ELEC CUE: 63)

(*Dance extension.*)

    BOTH.
IT'S LOVE MAKES THE WORLD GO ROUND

    BILL. (*As Al Jolson.*)
WITHOUT LOVE NOBODY WOULD SING
    SIR JOHN. (*As Bing Crosby.*)
WITHOUT LOVE NO WEDDING BELLS RING.
    (ELEC CUE: 64)

ANCESTORS.
AH ... AH ...
IT'S LOVE MAKES THE WORLD GO ROUND
AH ... AH ...
IT'S LOVE MAKES THE WORLD GO ROUND
SIR JOHN.
WITHOUT LOVE NOBODY WOULD SING
BILL.
WITHOUT LOVE ...
BILL & SIR JOHN.
NO WEDDING BELLS RING
ANCESTORS.
DING DONG
AH... AH...
AH... AH....
BILL AND SIR JOHN.
AND THOUGH PEOPLE DOUBT IT
THEY CAN'T LIVE WITHOUT IT
ALL OVER THE WORLD THEY'VE FOUND
BILL, SIR JOHN. ANCESTORS.
THAT LOVE MAKES THE WORLD GO ROUND
AND ROUND AND ROUND AND ROUND AND ROUND (ELEC CUE: 65)
AND ROUND AND ROUND AND ROUND AND ROUND

(To SIR JOHN's delight, BILL presents him with his watch as lights fade to black.) (ELEC CUE: 66)
(CREW CUE: 16)

Scene 3

[MUSIC CUE #19: LAMBETH UNDERSCORE]

Capstan Street, Lambeth.

ME AND MY GIRL

A street in Lambeth with a house, No. 21, and a pub. A barrel organ is heard playing "THE LAMBETH WALK".

[MUSIC CUE #19A: LAMBETH TAPE]

A TELEGRAPH BOY rides his bike to the door of No. 21, dismounts and knocks. VARIOUS LOCALS go about their business until the entrance of SIR JOHN.

(ELEC CUE: 67)

MRS. BROWN. (*Through the upstairs window.*) Yes?
BOY. Telegram for Miss Sally Smiff.
MRS. BROWN. Okay, little boy.
BOY. Any reply?
MRS. BROWN. She's not in.
BOY. Okay, big girl. (ELEC CUE: 68)

(*THE TELEGRAPH BOY puts the telegram through the letterbox and exits, left. SALLY enters up left followed by BOB BARKING with vegetable cart.*)

BOB. Oh come on, Sally!
SALLY. (*Crossing away, center.*) It's no use, Bob. I've got to give him his chance to be Lord Hareford.
BOB. (*Sets cart left, crosses center.*) Oh yeah, I see that, but what have you got to leave Lambeth for?
SALLY. Cos he'll only come after me 'ere if I don't. I've written him this letter telling 'im not to look for me cos 'e wont' find me.
BOB. Well, it seems all wrong to me.
MRS. BROWN. (*Entering from house.*) Sally love, there's a tellgrim come for you.
SALLY. (*Receiving telegram.*) For me. Oh I bet it's from Bill.
BOB. Is it?
SALLY. (*Handing BOB the telegram.*) What did I tell you?

BOB. (*Reading.*) "Stay put -- am fed up to the back teeth with being an earl, am throwing up everything and coming after. Love, Bill."

SALLY. Now you see why I've go to go. Goodbye, Bob. Keep your fingers crossed for me. (*Exit SALLY and MRS. BROWN into house.*)

BOB. (*Calling after SALLY.*) Good luck, Sally. (*Exit BOB into pub, passing GIRL.*) (ELEC CUE: 69)

(*Enter SIR JOHN up left to down right.*)

GIRL. Hello, Saucy.

SIR JOHN. What a good judge of character. Another time maybe.

(*CONSTABLE enters down right. GIRL exits up left.*)

SIR JOHN. Excuse me, can you tell me where I can find number Twenty-one Capstan Street?

CONSTABLE. (*In a perfect Oxford accent.*) For your information, Sir, you are already in Capstan Street, even as you ask, and by a further stretch of coincidence you find yourself immediately outside of number Twenty-one.

SIR JOHN. (*Amazed.*) Thank you, Officer.

CONSTABLE. Not at all, Sir. It gives me great satisfaction to be of any service. That is my function and I perform it with zeal.

SIR JOHN. Good Lord. Well, thank you. Dormez bien.

CONSTABLE. (*Crossing away, center.*) Merci bien, Monsieur. Bon soir et les beaux reves. (*Exits up right, behind the house.*) (ELEC CUE: 70)

SIR JOHN. An educated policeman! What next, a polite cabbie. Ah, here we are. Number Twenty-one. (*He knocks at the door. MRS. BROWN opens it.*)

MRS. BROWN. Yes?

ME AND MY GIRL

SIR JOHN. Good evening, Madam. Does Miss Sally Smith live here?

MRS. BROWN. Who wants her?

SIR JOHN. Well, say it's her fairy godfather.

MRS. BROWN. 'Er oo?

SIR JOHN. Just take me in to her.

MRS. BROWN. Oh, no you don't. Not in my house. Filthy beast! Sally! There's someone to see you.

SALLY. (*Offstage.*) Who is it?

MRS. BROWN. Says 'e's your furry godfather.

SIR JOHN. Fairy, not furry. (*Calling in.*) It's all right, Sally, it's only me.

SALLY. (*Offstage.*) Coming. (*She appears in the doorway.*) Sir John! What you doing here? (*MRS. BROWN is hovering inquisitively.*) It's all right, Mrs. Brown, this is a very dear friend of mine.

MRS. BROWN. I'm sure. This is what comes of 'obnobbing with the gentry.

SIR JOHN. Goodbye, fair spirit of morality.

(ELEC CUE: 71)

(*MRS. BROWN exits into the house, shutting the door.*)

SIR JOHN. Now, Sally, what's all this?

SALLY. (*Crossing downstage.*) It's not good, Sir John, I'm not going back. I'm going to move away. You're wasting your time.

SIR JOHN. (*Following.*) I haven't come here to persuade you to go back.

SALLY. You haven't?

SIR JOHN. No. We have to beat the duchess at her own game.

SALLY. The duchess don't like me. I'm not fit an' proper.

SIR JOHN. Ah, but suppose we *made* you fit and proper?

SALLY. (*Crossing below SIR JOHN to center.*) Get away. 'Sides I wouldn't want it.

SIR JOHN. It wouldn't do any harm. There are all kinds of things you can do with a good accent. Gerald has made a profession out of it for years. And look at Ronald Colman, Cary Grant...

SALLY. Yeah, I could get my little dress shop. I've always wanted to do that. but how would you do it?

SIR JOHN. Not me. But there's an army friend of mine. He shares a house in Upper Wimpole Street with a remarkable man who could certainly do it. He's done it before. If you love Bill, you'll let him try.

SALLY. Only if you promise not to tell Bill where I am.

SIR JOHN. I promise.

SALLY. Then we'd better go straight away, 'cos look. (*She shows him the telegram.*)

SIR JOHN. I'll give my friend a call.

SALLY. (*Crossing up to door.*) I'll run in and pack a few things.

SIR JOHN. (*Countering up left, center.*) Good girl. My car's at the end of the street.

(*SALLY opens the door and MRS. BROWN falls out. SALLY goes in.*)

MRS. BROWN. Ooh! Oh dear, I've dropped something.

SIR JOHN. A couple of eaves perhaps?

MRS. BROWN. Well, what if I was listening. It was for Sally's own good.

SIR JOHN. (*Crossing to MRS. BROWN.*) So you're Mrs. Brown.

MRS. BROWN. Mrs.Anastasia Brown, yes.

SIR JOHN. Well, Mrs. Anastasia Brown, you evidently heard that I'm going to take Sally away.

MRS. BROWN. Yes, I heard that fairy tale you was tellin' the poor mite.

SIR JOHN. But you also heard that she doesn't want Bill to know where she's gone. (*He takes out a five pound note.*)
MRS. BROWN. No more do you, I don't suppose.
SIR JOHN. (*Rustling the note.*) Do you know what this is, Mrs. Brown?
MRS. BROWN. It sounds like a fiver.
SIR JOHN. Does it look like a fiver?
MRS. BROWN. It is a five pound note.
SIR JOHN. (*Handing the note to her.*) Well done, Mrs. Brown. Here you are.
MRS. BROWN. Oooh thank you, sir.
SIR JOHN. Now there's more where that came from, if you keep your mouth shut when Bill comes for Sally.
MRS. BROWN. I get you, sir, mum's the word.
SIR JOHN. Good. Tell Sally I'll be waiting in the car. Farewell, Mrs. Anastasia Brown. (*To GIRL, as he exits.*) Not now, my dear. It's war, and I must rejoin my regiment. (*Exit SIR JOHN, up left. BILL enters up right behind the house.*)
MRS. BROWN. (*At her door.*) Oh my Gawd! I mean, oh my Lord.
BILL. Don't you start, Mrs. B. Where's Sally?
MRS. BROWN. She's gone. Not here. Gone.
BILL. (*Crossing left.*) Gone? Whatcher mean gone?
MRS. BROWN. (*Follows.*) She didn't say. She went away. Not coming back no more.
BILL. When?
MRS. BROWN. When? Ooh, ages ago.
BILL. 'Ere, did she get my wire then?
MRS. BROWN. Yes -- no ... I mean yes, that's what made her go.
BILL. She leave an address?
MRS. BROWN. No address.
BILL. What about her mail?
MRS. BROWN. (*Defeated, she crosses to house.*) Well, she'll collect it, I mean, I don't know.

BILL. (*Following.*) You telling me pork pies, Mrs. B. She in there?

MRS. BROWN. (*At door.*) No! She ain't! She's gone I tell you!

BILL. (*At lamppost.*) Oh yeah. I've heard that before. I'll wait 'ere.

MRS. BROWN. It's no good, Bill, she'll never come back.

BILL. Yeah? Well, we'll see about that. (*BILL leans against the lamppost, and MRS. BROWN goes indoors. the CONSTABLE reenters from left.*) (ELEC CUE: 72)

CONSTABLE. Now then, sir, I'm terribly afraid that you really can't stop here. [*MUSIC CUE #20: LEANING ON A LAMP-POST.*] It rather comes under the heading of loitering. Are you waiting for someone?

BILL.
LEANING ON A LAMP
MAYBE YOU THINK I LOOK A TRAMP
OR YOU MAY THINK I'M HANGING ROUND TO STEAL A CAR
BUT NO I'M NOT A CROOK
AND IF YOU THINK THAT'S WHAT I LOOK
I'LL TELL YOU WHY I'M HERE AND WHAT MY MOTIVES ARE

I'M LEANING ON A LAMP-POST
AT THE CORNER OF THE STREET
IN CASE A CERTAIN LITTLE LADY COMES BY
OH ME, OH MY, I HOPE THE LITTLE LADY COMES BY
(*CONSTABLE exits, left.*)

I DON'T KNOW IF SHE'LL GET AWAY
SHE DOESN'T ALWAYS GET AWAY
BUT ANYWAY I KNOW THAT SHE'LL TRY
OH ME, OH MY, I HOPE THE LITTLE LADY COMES BY

ME AND MY GIRL

THERE'S NO OTHER GIRL I WOULD WAIT FOR
BUT THIS ONE I'D BREAK ANY DATE FOR I WON'T
   HAVE TO ASK WHAT SHE'S LATE FOR
SHE WOULDN'T LEAVE ME FLAT
SHE'S NOT A GIRL LIKE THAT
SHE'S ABSOLUTELY WONDERFUL
AND MARVELOUS AND BEAUTIFUL
AND ANYONE CAN UNDERSTAND WHY --

I'M LEANING ON A LAMP-POST
AT THE CORNER OF THE STREET
IN CASE A CERTAIN LITTLE LADY COMES BY

(ELEC CUE: 73)

"THE LAMBETH BALLET"

(ELEC CUE: 74)

(BILL stands leaning on the lamp-post. BOB BARKING enters from the pub and crosses left, to his vegetable cart. BILL crosses to him, and they exchange greetings. Soon YOUNG MEN OF LAMBETH enter and dance with BILL. When LAMBETH LADIES arrive and couple with YOUNG MEN, BILL is alone. He fantasizes SALLY as they dance in a dream-like setting. As BILL sweeps SALLY into his arms, reality returns. SALLY is gone, and BILL is renewed.)

(ELEC CUE: 76)

BILL.
THERE'S NO OTHER GIRL I WOULD WAIT FOR
BUT THIS ONE I'D BREAK ANY DATE FOR I WON'T
   HAVE TO ASK WHAT SHE'S LATE FOR
SHE WOULDN'T LEAVE ME FLAT
SHE'S NOT A GIRL LIKE THAT

SHE'S ABSOLUTELY WONDERFUL
AND MARVELOUS AND BEAUTIFUL
AND ANYONE CAN UNDERSTAND WHY --
I'M LEANING ON A LAMP-POST

AT THE CORNER OF THE STREET
IN CASE A CERTAIN LITTLE LADY COMES BY

(ELEC CUE: 77)

(BILL is alone leaning on the lamp-post by SALLY's door. MRS. BROWN comes out of the doorway and hands BILL a note. She exits.)

[MUSIC CUE# 20A: LAMP-POST TAG]

BILL.
I'M LEANING ON A LAMP-POST
AT THE CORNER OF THE STREET
IN CASE A CERTAIN LITTLE LADY...

(BILL crumples the note and throws it into the trash can. He blows out the lamp and the scene blacks out.)

(ELEC CUE: 79)
(CREW CUE: 17)

(ELEC CUE: 80)
(CREW CUE: 18)

Scene 4

[MUSIC CUE #21: THE HUNT BALL]

The Hunt Ball, Hareford Hall.
The set begins it's transformation from Lambeth to Hareford Hall as Ball GUESTS swirl onstage dancing. Suddenly an intoxicated BILL enters through the upstage doors. He crosses down center and exits left followed by an assisting HETHERSETT. As the dance ends, GUESTS exit. [MUSIC CUE #21: COCKTAIL MUSIC] *The DUCHESS enters down left followed by LADY BATTERSBY, LADY DISS, and LORD BATTERSBY. SIR JOHN enters up right and crosses center to greet the DUCHESS. During LORD, LADIES*

meet SIR JASPER on upstage steps and exit to the terrace.

SIR JOHN. How now, Maria. You've been moping for days. What's the matter, bad news from your bookmaker.

(LORD and LADIES laugh as they exit. HETHERSETT enters up right with champagne glasses on tray.)

DUCHESS. Oh, John, I just despair of Bill. Since Sally went away he has become impossible. He's wasted thousands on detectives to look for her, newspaper advertisements, offering huge rewards. Nothing.

(HETHERSETT offers champagne to DUCHESS and SIR JOHN. They decline. HETHERSETT exits up right.)

DUCHESS. And he's convinced that I know where she is. I could almost wish the wretched girl back here.
SIR JOHN. Ah, well, you never know. Perhaps she will come back. Stranger things have happened.
DUCHESS. *(Turning away.)* It's so dispiriting.
SIR JOHN. *(Countering above her.)* Well, Maria, I never thought I'd say it, but I preferred you when you were a ghastly old trout. Do cheer up.
DUCHESS. Usually, I buy myself a new hat when I'm down in the dumps.
SIR JOHN. So that's where you get them from.
DUCHESS. *(Crossing away, right.)* I never realized how truly fond of her Bill is. I thought when she was out of the way... but he's done nothing but sulk.
SIR JOHN. I know, he's just not the same is he. *(Showing his gold watch.)* But, it's never too late. I knew a couple once who had secretly loved each other for thirty years.
DUCHESS. *(Turning back.)* Thirty years?

SIR JOHN. Thirty-one years, seven months and three days. Their love was so secret that they weren't even aware of it themselves.
DUCHESS. And what happened?
SIR JOHN. (*Gingerly crossing to DUCHESS.*) Well, they struggled miserably along...until one day the man took it into his head...after all this time, to get down on one knee, not unlike this, and say in his simple, direct, manly way, "I can't move."
DUCHESS. I can't move?
SIR JOHN. Dammit, Maria, my leg's seized up. Hit my back. Higher. Left a bit. Harder. That's it.
DUCHESS. Oh, John. (*Standing.*)
SIR JOHN. Damned shrapnel. Always gives a twinge when I get worked up. Where was I?
DUCHESS. This couple. The man was about to propose.
SIR JOHN. Oh, Maria... (*He bends to kiss her. HETHERSETT enters.*)
DUCHESS. Oh, John. (*HETHERSETT clears his throat. DUCHESS points to HETHERSETT, but SIR JOHN thinking they are still alone takes the gesture as an indication of "going upstairs." He points to the balcony. The DUCHESS is shocked.*) No, no, no!
SIR JOHN. What?

(*HETHERSETT coughs.*)

DUCHESS. I shall got for a walk in the garden. (*DUCHESS exits down left. HETHERSETT steps down left center.*)
SIR JOHN. Good heavens, Hethersett, you here?
HETHERSETT. Yes, Sir.
SIR JOHN. Women, Hethersett.
HETHERSETT. Yes, Sir.
SIR JOHN. (*Crosses to HETHERSETT.*) You ever been in love, Hethersett?
HETHERSETT. Oh, no, Sir. I'm married.

SIR JOHN. Really? I had no idea.
HETHERSETT. To the cook, Sir. You were kind enough to attend the ceremony.
SIR JOHN. Was I? Be that as it may...Is she here yet?
HETHERSETT. Beg your pardon?
SIR JOHN. Is she here yet?
HETHERSETT. Oh, yes, Sir. I put her where you told me to.
SIR JOHN. What?
HETHERSETT. I put her where you told me to.
SIR JOHN. Sshhhh... Good, man. And remember, not a word to anyone.
PARCHESTER. (*Enters upstage.*) Everything going according to plan, Sir John?
SIR JOHN & HETHERSETT. Shhhh ... (*SIR JOHN and PARCHESTER exit down right. HETHERSETT crosses right to adjust chair. JAQUIE and GERALD enter up left.*)
JAQUIE. (*Crossing to HETHERSETT.*) Hethersett. Where's Lord Hareford?
HETHERSETT. I believe he is in his bedroom, Lady Jaqueline.
JAQUIE. Bedroom? What's he doing?
HETHERSETT. I believe he is packing, my Lady.
JAQUIE. Packing? What on earth is he packing for?
HETHERSETT. (*Crossing to left chair.*) He did not confide in me, my Lady.
GERALD. I told you so.
JAQUIE. I'm going to have it out with him once and for all.
GERALD. Jaquie, you're not going into his bedroom?
JAQUIE. No, perhaps you're right. Hethersett.
HETHERSETT. My Lady.
JAQUIE. Ask Lord Hareford to come here please.
HETHERSETT. Very good, my Lady. (*HETHERSETT exits left. JAQUIE begins to pace around the stage. GERALD follows.*)

GERALD. Well, frankly, Jaquie, you're making a complete ass of yourself, chasing after Bill Hareford after all these months. You know perfectly well he's done nothing but search for Sally. And even now when he's threatening to go back to Lambeth, still you pertain.

JAQUIE. No, still you persist.

GERALD. I will not persist. I shall carry on until you give up this nonsense and marry me. (*He kneels.*)

JAQUIE. Marry you? With all your debts? Ha!

GERALD. Well as a matter of fact I don't have any debts. Bill was good enough to write me a big check...

(*BILL enters up left and crosses center. He is dressed in his Cockney clothes.*)

BILL. Olly! Olly! All fresh! Ripe strawberries! You rang, Madam. (*Tosses his hat offstage.*)

DUCHESS. (*Enters down right, wearing BILL's hat.*) What is the meaning of this?

JAQUIE. (*Crossing to BILL.*) Oh, Mummy! Oh, William, you're not really packing to go.

BILL. And what's more I am going. Until the duchess produces Sally!

DUCHESS. How many times do I have to tell you ...

JAQUIE. Sally! Sally! And what about me! I'm not to be cast aside lightly.

BILL. No, you should be thrown with great force.

JAQUIE. But don't you feel something when we're together?

BILL. I feel ill.

JAQUIE. But I though you cared for me.

BILL. I couldn't care for you. I'm just an ordinary earl, not a vet.

JAQUIE. Let me tell you, I wouldn't marry you now if you were the last man on earth.

BILL. If I were the last man on earth I'd be too busy to marry anybody.

JAQUIE. (*Slaps BILL and exits up left.*) Oh!

ME AND MY GIRL

GERALD. (*Crosses to BILL.*) I say, that was a slap in the face. It would have served her right if you'd slapped her in the face.
BILL. It's not her face wants slapping.
GERALD. Yes, but you couldn't very well...
BILL. No? She'd marry the first man who does.
GERALD. She will? I say do you really think so? I'd never thought of that. (*GERALD exits up left with determination.*)
DUCHESS. William, where are you planning to go?
BILL. Lambeth, Auntie.
DUCHESS. Oh, but this is madness, madness.

(*There is a slap offstage.*)

JAQUIE. (*Offstage.*) Ooh!
DUCHESS. Haven't I done enough for you, haven't I thrown parties for you?
BILL. At me.

(*Another slap is heard.*)

DUCHESS. You must have a son to insure the succession. Better still, lots of sons.
BILL. You've got a mind like a gerbil.
DUCHESS. Well, you can't go now, not after all I've achieved.
BILL. I can if you don't tell me where Sally is.
DUCHESS. But I don't know where she is.

(*Another slap offstage.*)

JAQUIE. (*Offstage.*) Ooh, Gerald!
BILL. Then tomorrow every picture palace in London'll show a newsreel of Lord Hareford going back to Lambeth.

(*Enter GERALD and JAQUIE, who is rather flushed.*)

GERALD. I say, I say, you'll never guess what's happened. Jaqueline has promised to be my trouble and strife.

BILL. Asshh! Sorry. And now I'm going back to Lambeth to make Sally be my wife.

DUCHESS. And to make the same mistake as your father.

BILL. The only mistake he made was to leave his girl. I shan't. I'm sorry, Auntie Duchess, you seem to have lost your little battle.

DUCHESS. I hope I'm not ungracious in defeat. You may kiss your aunt.

BILL. No, you may kiss your nevvie.

(*SIR JOHN, PARCHESTER, SIR JASPER enter down right in time to see the DUCHESS kiss BILL on the cheek.*)

DUCHESS. Goodbye, Bill. You're a true Hareford.

BILL. Right! I'm off to finish packing. Cheerio, everybody. (*BILL exits up left. SIR JOHN runs center.*)

SIR JOHN. Gerald, go and fetch him back, quick.

GERALD. What for?

SIR JOHN. You'll see.

(*GERALD exits up left. SIR JOHN grabs SIR JASPER's ear trumpet and blows it as a horn. BATTERSBYS and GUESTS rush on. HETHERSETT enters up center, announcing.*)

HETHERSETT. Miss Sally Smith.

[MUSIC Cue #23: SALLY'S ENTRANCE]

DUCHESS. Who?

JAQUIE. What?

SALLY. (*Enters up center in dress and action very much a lady. She holds a large feather fan. Curtseying to DUCHESS.*) How do you do, your Grace? Lady Jaqueline? Such a pleasure. Gentlemen.
SIR JOHN. I think she's got it.
DUCHESS. What does this mean?
SALLY. (*Crossing down center.*) We're all of us susceptible to the right treatment, your Grace.
DUCHESS. You, John.

(*SIR JOHN bows.*)

DUCHESS. John, you ... Oh, my goodness, Sally. Does Bill know?
SALLY. Not yet.
GERALD. (*Runs in from up left and crosses down right to PARCHESTER. Announcing.*) He's on his way.

(*BILL enters up left with two tattered suitcases. He crosses down left to the DUCHESS.*)

SIR JOHN. William, my boy. I would like you to meet a special little friend of mine.
SALLY. (*Hiding her face behind her fan.*) How do you do, Lord Hareford.
BILL. How do you do? Charlie, get the car round please.

(*HETHERSETT exits.*)

SALLY. Do I take it that you are going somewhere, Lord Hareford? What are those two bags doing? (*She points at the cases in front of the DUCHESS and JAQUIE.*)
BILL. They live here. (*Crosses up to the foot of the staircase.*)
SALLY. (*Following.*) Back to Lambeth, I understand.
BILL. That's right, yeah. To find Sally.

SALLY. It seems to me, Lord Hareford, and you'll forgive me for saying so, that you must be extremely fond of this girl to give everything up for her like this.

BILL. If you only knew how much I wanted her to come back.

SALLY. And if she does come back, Lord Hareford, what on earth will you say to her after all this time?

BILL. What'll I say? What'll I say? I'll say... I'll say...

(SALLY lowers her fan.)

BILL. *(Seeing SALLY.)* Where the bloody hell have you been?

[MUSIC CUE #24: FINALE]

*(BILL and SALLY embrace to everyone's delight. **Blackout.**)*

(ELEC CUE: 82)
(CREW CUE: 19)

(CREW CUE: 20)
(ELEC CUE: 83)

Scene 5

Hareford Hall.
The Wedding Reception.
The GUESTS, COCKNEYS, and STAFF greet the WEDDING COUPLES: JAQUIE and GERALD, DUCHESS and SIR JOHN, and BILL AND SALLY. They sing.

GUESTS, COCKNEYS, STAFF.
WITHOUT LOVE NOBODY WOULD SING

WITHOUT LOVE NO WEDDING BELLS RING
THE WORLD KEEPS ON TURNING
YOU CAN'T STOP IT TURNING
FOR LOVE MAKES THE WORLD GO ROUND

AN OLD LOVE A NEW LOVE
SO LONG AS IT'S TRUE LOVE
IT'S LOVE MAKES THE WORLD GO ROUND
WITHOUT LOVE NOBODY WOULD SING
WITHOUT LOVE NO WEDDING BELLS RING

AND THOUGH PEOPLE DOUBT IT
THEY CAN'T LIVE WITHOUT IT
ALL OVER THE WORLD THEY'VE FOUND
THAT LOVE MAKES THE WORLD GO ROUND

(ELEC CUE: 84)

BILL, SALLY, DUCHESS, SIR JOHN, JAQUIE, GERALD.
ME AND MY GIRL, MEANT FOR EACH OTHER
SENT FOR EACH OTHER, AND LIKING IT SO
ME AND MY GIRL, IT'S NO USE PRETENDING
WE KNEW THE ENDING A LONG TIME AGO

SOME LITTLE CHURCH, WITH A BIG STEEPLE
JUST A FEW PEOPLE THAT BOTH OF US KNOW

ALL.
AND WE'LL HAVE LOVE -- LAUGHTER
BE HAPPY EVER AFTER, ME AND MY GIRL

(ELEC CUE: 85)

(Direct segue to curtain calls.)

[MUSIC CUE #25: BOWS]

(OPT CREW CUE: 21)
(OPT ELEC CUE: 86)

REPRISE: "LAMBETH WALK"

ALL.
ANY TIME YOU'RE LAMBETH WAY

ANY EVENING -- ANY DAY
YOU'LL FIND US ALL
DOING THE LAMBETH WALK

EVERY LITTLE LAMBETH GAL
WITH HER LITTLE LAMBETH PAL
YOU'LL FIND US ALL
DOING THE LAMBETH WALK

EVERYTHING FREE AND EASY
DO AS YOU DARN WELL PLEASEY
WHY DON'T YOU MAKE YOUR WAY THERE
GO THERE -- STAY THERE

ONCE YOU GET DOWN LAMBETH WAY
EVERY EVENING -- EVERY DAY
YOU'LL FIND YOURSELF
DOING THE LAMBETH
DOING THE LAMBETH WALK -- OI

(CREW CUE: 22)
(ELEC CUE: 87)

CURTAIN

[MUSIC CUE #26: PLAYOUT]

ME AND MY GIRL

OPERATING NOTES

The following informational guide has been modified from the Broadway production, and corresponds to the script and ground plan in this edition.

ACT I
PRESET: SHOW DROP
                 EFFECTS SCRIM
                 FOLIAGE DROPS
                 TREES
                 CYC

CAR, a prop unit made up of several pieces of luggage, running board, revolving tires, windshield, steering wheel, splits center behind Effects Scrim and in front of closed GATES
GATES CLOSED (on)
HOUSE TURNTABLE, above gates and in exterior position.

CUES: (See Script)

1) SHOW DROP out
2) EFFECTS SCRIM out
3) GATES OPEN (off)
4) HOUSE moves to downstage position
5) HOUSE revolves to interior position
   FOLIAGE DROPS out
   TREES out
   DOWNSTAGE ARCH in
   CHANDELIERS in
   UPSTAGE ARCH in
6) HOUSE upstage to storage
   DOWNSTAGE ARCH out
   CHANDELIERS out
   UPSTAGE ARCH out
   RIGHT & LEFT KITCHEN UNITS on

KITCHEN FLAT in

During I-2: crew presets HOUSE to exterior position and brings in DRAWING ROOM DROP. Crew operates kitchen bell as per orchestration.

7) KITCHEN FLAT out
RIGHT & LEFT KITCHEN UNITS off

DRAWING ROOM DROP is momentarily revealed by itself. STAFF strikes kitchen props and sets DRAWING ROOM props: sofa, accent table, desk and chair.
    DOWNSTAGE ARCH in
    DRAWING ROOM WINGS in
    DRAWING ROOM FLAT in

8) DOWNSTAGE ARCH out
DRAWING ROOM WINGS out
STAFF strikes sofa and desk/chair above PUB FLAT location

9) PUB FLAT in
LOCALS set piano, piano stool, pub bench
During I-4:
DRAWING ROOM FLAT out
DRAWING ROOM DROP out

Crew sets HOUSE directly above PUB FLAT, set whiskey bar, right, and party table, left. Right and left escape stairs align with HOUSE balcony. Drawing room props off. FAMILY "dressing" props set at balcony windows.
    FUGUE DROP in
    FOLIAGE in
    TREES in

10) PUB FLAT out

ME AND MY GIRL

        Crew strikes pub props. STAFF moves bar and party table downstage to enlarge the playing area.

11)   SHOW DROP in

ACT II
PRESET:

    HOUSE to up right playing position; exterior view. HOUSE MASKING FLATS, GARDEN WALL WITH ARCH set about HOUSE area. Garden table with three chairs, right, garden ladder, left, 2 lawn chairs, left center. RIGHT AND LEFT GARDEN PLINTHS set in #2. Strike RIGHT KITCHEN UNIT from preset position and set LAMBETH HOUSE in its place.

    FOLIAGE DROPS in
    TREES in
    CYC in
    During scene STAFF moves garden table and chairs to down right location.

12)   FOLIAGE DROPS out
    TREES out
    DOWNSTAGE ARCH in
    LIBRARY FLAT in

    Crew sets: Library sliders on, round table & library ladder, left. Tiger skin down center with strike line off right, Ancestor book with stand on right "garden" table. Crew strikes all garden props. RIGHT and LEFT PLINTHS off. Note: actor playing BILL sets library chair since scene begins with cape caught under chair leg. LIBRARY FLAT plays in front of II-1 HOUSE and

WALL positions. Escape stairs align with LIBRARY FLAT.

During scene: Crew sets HOUSE up center in storage position, interior view, and strikes II-1 props. Crew presets LAMPPOST/FENCE unit in right #2.

13) Cue tiger off
14) LIBRARY FLAT FRAMES down to lower body position
15) LIBRARY FLAT FRAMES restore to upper body position

Note: During "SONG OF HAREFORD" and "LOVES MAKES THE WORLD GO ROUND" crew operates the mouths of the library busts as if they were singing chorus vocals.

16) DOWNSTAGE ARCH out
LIBRARY FLAT out
LAMBETH ARCH in
LAMBETH FLAT in
LAMBETH DROP in
LAMPPOST/FENCE in
LAMBETH HOUSE on
Crew strikes II-2 props
Stage smoke provides Lambeth fog effect
During scene: Dry ice employed in ballet dream sequence

17) LAMBETH DROP out
LAMBETH FLAT out
LAMBETH ARCH out
LAMPPOST/FENCE off
LAMBETH HOUSE off
Crew strikes II-3 props
HOUSE interior seen against starlit cyc.

18) HOUSE moves to downstage position
DOWNSTAGE ARCH in
CHANDELIERS in
UPSTAGE ARCH in

ME AND MY GIRL 113

          FOOTMEN set armchair in front of each
          DOWNSTAGE ARCH column

19)   SHOW DROP in
          Crew strikes armchairs, suitcases
20)   SHOW DROP out
21)   Optional change to exterior during
          "LAMBETH WALK" reprise.
          DOWNSTAGE ARCH out
          CHANDELIERS out
          UPSTAGE ARCH out
          FOLIAGE in
          TREES in
          HOUSE revolves to exterior position
22)   SHOW DROP in

LIGHTING NOTES

The lighting of ME AND MY GIRL is traditional. The following informational guide has been modified from the Broadway production, and corresponds to the electrical cues in this script.

CUE: DESCRIPTION:

1)   Lights behind scrim reveal GUESTS in and about car
2)   Car in motion. Effects projectors on scrim and/or additional motion effect lighting behind scrim
3)   Car "stops". Effects scrim out. Add front fill
4)   Build. Warm exterior, summer
5)   Exterior to interior. Bright. Show exterior grounds and sky thru windows. Attention to set's architectural detail
6)   Balcony area up for GERALD

7) Balcony area down
8) Adjust for scene
9) Adjust for musical number
10) Restore for scene. Generally bright and clean
11) Build for musical number
12) Restore for scene
13) BILL and SALLY scene. Soften and warm up. Later in the afternoon
14) Adjust for song
15) Build for dance
16) Adjust down for two
17) Restore Cue 10
18) Fade to black holding BILL and SALLY on stairs until last moment. Optional cue reveals "interesting" details of set change
19) Kitchen interior. No windows. Incandescent feeling as light reflects off kitchen wall tiles, stone and white kitchen furnishing.
20) Adjust for scene
21) Lighting down except for SERVANTS area down center
22) Build lighting for drawing room. A brightly lit area on a warm summer's day. Show grounds and sky thru windows
23) Adjust for musical number
24) Restore for scene
25) Down for BILL and SALLY on sofa
26) Build for dance extension
27) Restore for scene
28) Fade all, but down left area for BILL and HETHERSETT
29) The Pub, in one. Dimly lit. No windows. Sconces by bench and piano provide "source." Effects projector provides fireplace reflection to warm left area
30) Lights fade to black

ME AND MY GIRL

32) The Terrace, early evening. Cool, comfortable, shadows. Warm lighting from interior thru windows and doors Focus on FAMILY windows
33) Begin general build
34) Fade FAMILY windows
35) Build downstage playing area
36) Build for Cockney entrance
37) Adjust for song
38) Build for dance
39) Fade down to house area. Night all around as GUESTS enter warmly lit house
40) Blackout
41) A bright, sunny, afternoon
42) Adjust for tap break
43) Adjust for vocal
44) Down a bit for scene
45) Adjust for vocal
46) Blackout
47) Library interior. Late afternoon light shafts from high windows out of sight. Warm, rich feeling.
48) Down for SALLY at round table, right
49) Restore Cue 47
50) Lighting and light adjustment as one ANCESTOR portrait is lit and "scrims-thru"
51) Portrait out. Restore 47
52) Lightning and light adjustment as second ANCESTOR portrait is lit and "scrims-thru"
53) Second ANCESTOR out. Third ANCESTOR up.
54) All ANCESTOR portraits light. Light bookcase busts.
55) Adjust for song as ANCESTOR portraits fade out.
56) ANCESTOR portraits up.

57)	Portrait frames lower to reveal ANCESTOR feet. Light accordingly
57a)	ANCESTOR portrait lights out
58)	ANCESTORS enter. A sense of the fantastic.
59)	Build color for end
60)	Adjust for reprise
61)	Restore Cue 47
62)	Adjust for song
63)	Build for dance extension
64)	Add ANCESTOR portraits and bookcase busts
65)	Fade all but BILL and SIR JOHN at left chair
66)	Blackout
67)	Lambeth. Dark and smoky. Lamplighter lights two street lamps as lights come up. Light from Mrs. Brown's windows and upstage pub
68)	Build lighting in left center area
69)	Build light in right center area
70)	Build light in Mrs. Brown's area
71)	Build lighting downstage
72)	Adjust down for song
73)	Adjustment as MEN enter
74)	Adjustment as WOMEN enter
75)	Adjust for BILL's fantasy
76)	Restore Cue 72
77)	Adjustment as Dancers exit
78)	Down for BILL. Secondary lamppost out
79)	BILL blows out the lamppost. Blackout
80)	Scene segue. Hunt Ball. Much color
81)	Interior. Night. Brightly lit. Exterior: stars and lighted reflecting pool is seen thru doors and windows
82)	Blackout
83)	Brightly lit area. Afternoon. Grounds and sky seen thru windows

ME AND MY GIRL

84) Down to highlight three couples
85) Restore CUE 83
86) Optional if set changes to garden exterior for "Lambeth Walk;" Exterior, evening
87) Curtain. Fronts down

PROPERTY PRESETS

STAGE RIGHT

I-1   3 Umbrellas (STOCKBROKERS)
3 Briefcases (STOCKBROKERS)
Well abused briefcases (PARCHESTER)
Buffet table with cloth to floor, grandly dressed with candelabra, champagne bucket, silver cigarette box with cigarettes, London Times, pheasant on silver tray, "200 year old" decanter, vase of flowers with 3 "Family Solicitor" trick flowers, additional food and ornamental dressing
Accent table with vase of flowers and letter rack
3 side chairs (HOUSE STAFF)

I-2   Vegetable basket with real celery, carrots (GARDENER)
Cutting board with cleaver, knife, knife sharpener, piece of meat (CHEF)
Hutch with two dish cloths, dustpan, brush, 6 glasses, sherry
Wooden tray with cups and saucers, pepper mill, teapot, silverware

I-3   2 Small books (JAQUIE)
5 Tennis rackets (DANCERS)
Sofa with 2 pillows; one containing paper projectile

	Accent table with flowers, dressing Invitations (DUCHESS) Brown legal folder with 3 letters (PARCHESTER)
I-4	Beer steins (SIR JOHN, SALLY, LOCALS) Piano Piano stool
I-5	I-1 Buffet table dressed as whiskey bar with champagne glasses, soda glasses, punch bowl, orange, lemons, cutting board, additional dressing Brass music stand (STAGE VIOLINIST)
II-1	Picnic basket with champagne glasses, napkins, etc. (GUESTS) Car blanket, pillow (GUESTS) Round table with cloth, 3 cups and saucers, cake and fork on plate for PARCHESTER Silver coffee service, cups/saucers (MAID)
II-2	Ancestor book with "Family tree" Book stand Tiger rug Library chair Sword (BILL)
II-3	Net bag with fruit (LOCAL X-OVER) Lamplighter's lighting torch (LAMPLIGHTER) Laundry basket with rags (LAMBETH RAG LADY) Tramp's bundle of clothes (LAMBETH TRAMP)

ME AND MY GIRL

II-4 Silver tray with three champagne glasses (HETHERSETT)
Hunting horn (used as JASPER's ear trumpet in this scene) (SIR JASPER)

II-5 Photographer's professional camera (PHOTOGRAPHER)
Party streamers (GUESTS)
Bridal bouquet (SALLY)

STAGE RIGHT UNITS

KITCHEN UNIT:
Galley tray with BILL's lunch leftovers set in dumbwaiter
Tea kettle, dishtowel, scrub brush, silverware in and around sink area

LAMBETH HOUSE:
Milk bottle, tea kettle, telegram, SALLY's note for BILL (Mrs. Brown)

STAGE LEFT

I-1 Small dinner gong and striker (GERALD)
Small silver tray to be used to present wine to SALLY (FOOTMAN)
2 Armchairs (HOUSE STAFF)
2 Straight chairs (HOUSE STAFF)
Buffet table grandly dressed with cloth to floor, candelabra, silver candy dish, silver tray with wine decanter, whiskey decanter, wine glasses, whiskey glasses, additional food and flower dressing
2 Armchairs
Side chair

I-2   Fridge with 2 drinking glasses, small pitcher with water, bowl of ice, bottle of beer, food dressing
Copper trash bin with stored champagne bottle
Riding crop (BILL)
Kitchen props: cutting board, sugar/creamer, knife, 2 mixing bowls, 2 eggs and beater in bowl (STAFF)

I-3   Drawing room desk with desk blotter, inkwell, phone, cigarette box with cigarettes, ashtray, matches, bud vase with flower, handbell, dressing
Cricket bat (GERALD)
Cricket pads, hat (DANCERS for BILL)
Tennis racket (DANCER)

I-4   Shotgun (FOOTMAN for BILL)
Tray with mug and bar rag (BAR MAN)

I-5   Pearly King's umbrella
Large silver tray with canapes (MAID)
Oval silver tray with canapes (WAITER)
Family "Fugue" props: 2 hand mirrors, 3 atomizers, 1 powder puff, 1 hair brush
Round "party" table with 3 apples, canapes, fruit bowl, 6 pairs of spoons, additional dressing

II-1   2 Croquet mallets and balls (JAQUIE, GERALD)
Croquet mallet and ball (DUCHESS)
Pocket whiskey flask (SIR JOHN)
Mallet (SIR JOHN)
Hedge clippers (GARDENER)
Garden ladder (GARDENER)
2 Fashion magazines (GUESTS)

ME AND MY GIRL 121

        Suitcase (SALLY)

II-2   Round table (I-5 party table) with tray of 2 whiskey decanters, 2 soda glasses, bud vase with flower
Rolling library ladder
2 Ancestor banners (ANCESTORS)
Tea cart with tea service, cups and saucers, tea sandwiches, additional dressing

II-3   Vegetable cart (BOB BARKING)
Bicycle, telegram (TELEGRAPH BOY)
Bicycle (LOCAL)
Trash can, crate, whiskey bottle (LOCAL TRAMP)
Umbrella (SIR JOHN)
Fruit basket (LOCAL)
Flashlight, notebook, pencil (CONSTABLE)
Shopping basket (SALLY)
Sally's letter (SALLY)

II-4   Champagne bottle (BILL)
Cigars (GUESTS)
2 Tattered suitcases (BILL)
Champagne glasses (FAMILY, GUESTS)

II-5   2 Wedding bouquets
Party streamers

STAGE LEFT UNITS

KITCHEN UNIT
Apple pie, large soup pot on stove

COSTUME PLOT

BILL SNIBSON

I-1 Distressed and soiled black and white checked two piece suit, brown bowler hat, grey waistcoat, white collarless shirt, white knee length socks, black oxford shoes, red/white spotted necktie, red/white spotted hankie.
Black shoes with taps for second entrance

I-2 Brown riding jacket, riding breeches, black riding boots, cream wing collar shirt, tattersall waistcoat, cream stock and pearl tie-pin, black bowler hat

I-3 As I-2

I-4 As I-2 plus deerstalker hat, riding mac

I-5 Single breasted white dinner jacket with red carnation, pique front shirt, wing collar, black bow tie, black shoes, black socks, black evening trousers, waistcoat to match, black bowler hat (worn to stage by COCKNEY DANCER)

II-2 Grey matching waistcoat and flannels, blue stripe shirt, navy blue tie, black shoes and socks, red velvet, ermine-trimmed cape, coronet

II-3 Black tails, black evening trousers, white wing collar shirt, white waistcoat, white bow tie, black patent shoes, black socks, raincoat

ME AND MY GIRL

II-4   Red tails, black evening trousers, white waistcoat, black patent shoes, black socks, white bow tie.
As in I-1 for second entrance

II-5   Grey morning suit with white carnation, grey waistcoat, grey trousers, white wing collar shirt, grey cravat, pearl pin, grey top hat, black shoes, grey gloves.

SALLY SMITH

I-1   Red/white floral shirtwaist dress, red beret, brown shoes with taps, red clutch bag, cream knickers (throughout), white petticoat, seamed cotton lisle stockings and garter belt (thru II-3)

I-3   Add cream linen jacket, brown shoes (no taps)

I-4   As above

I-5   Black/white spotted dress, orange shoes with purple bows, red feather boa, black hat with ostrich feathers, white petticoat and flounced hem

II-1   Blue floral dress, brown shoes, cream linen jacket

II-2   As II-1

II-3   As II-1
Dream ballet: Red organdy copy of I-5 dress, brown shoes

II-4	White gold beaded evening dress, white satin shoes, diamond tiara, bracelet, earrings, necklace, ostrich feather fan, white evening gloves
II-5	White wedding dress, shoes, veil, bouquet, evening gloves

MARIA, DUCHESS OF DENE

I-1	Peacock blue pleated skirt, jacket, beige shoes, pearl necklace, pearl earrings, emerald/diamond ring, silver wrist watch, cameo brooch (attached to dress), seamed stockings throughout
I-3	Eau de nil dress and jacket, pale green shoes, guipure lace blouse, previous jewelry, diamond brooch attached to dress
I-5	Grey/silver beaded evening dress, grey shoes, small diamond tiara, diamond pearl necklace, earrings, pale pink corsage, diamond brooch attached to dress, white evening gloves
II-1	Green/white silk dress, jacket, blouse, green/white floral picture hat, pale green shoes, jewelry as before, third different diamond brooch, short white gloves, lorgnette
II-2	As II-1 without hat and gloves
II-4	Black/bronze evening dress, black shoes, white gloves, large diamond tiara, brooch, bracelet, earrings, white fox fur stole

II-5 Grey lace wedding dress and jacket, grey shoes, grey/pink organza hat and roses, white/silver bouquet, white evening gloves

LADY JAQUELINE CARSTONE

I-1 Salmon jacket, dress, white shoes, gold bracelet watch (throughout), pearl earrings, emerald, diamond ring, seamed stockings

I-3 Peach teddy with matching under-brief, blue satin robe, silver shoes with white maribou poofs, pearl earrings

I-5 Peach robe with feather trim, gold evening dress, gold shoes, lotus flower diamond headdress with gold feathers, white evening gloves, pearl/gold/diamond bracelet, diamond earrings, necklace

II-1 Green floral print dress with flounce, green and white tap shoes, green straw hat, pearl necklace, 2 green bangle bracelets, pearl and diamond earrings, 2 stone rings

II-2 As II-1 without hat

II-4 Red/gold evening dress with bird wing back, white feather boa, white gloves, red shoes, large diamond earrings

II-5 White wedding dress, white shoes, white veil attached to white wreath and pink/white bouquet. Ring as in I-1

SIR JOHN TREMAYNE

I-1   Brown three piece suit, brown striped shirt with white wing collar, red paisley bow tie and pocket square, brown shoes, beige socks, signet ring, double watch chain and fob (throughout), gold hunter watch preset in BILL's waistcoat)

I-3   As I-1, but different waistcoat (yellow), white wing collar shirt, brown bow tie and pocket square

I-4   Raincoat, brown felt fedora, red paisley scarf (Over I-5 clothes)

I-5   Black double breasted dinner jacket, black evening trousers, white wing collar shirt, black bow tie, shoes, socks

II-1   Cream jacket, light brown trousers, matching double breasted waistcoat, brown shoes, socks, wing collar shirt, yellow bow tie and pocket square, straw hat

II-2   As II-1 without hat

II-3   As I-5 with white evening scarf

II-4   Black tails, evening trousers, black patent shoes, wing collar, shirt, white waistcoat, white bow tie, white gloves

II-5   Grey morning coat, white carnation, grey waistcoat, grey trousers black shoes, grey gloves, grey cravat and pin, grey top hat

THE HON. GERALD BOLINGBROKE

I-1 Striped dressing gown, red cravat over beige plus fours, argyle sleeveless top, (beige/brown natural), matching knee socks, brown shoes, striped shirt, tortoise shell spectacles and gold wrist watch throughout

I-3 White shirt, white pants, cricket hat, sweater, pads, gloves, shoes

I-5 White dinner jacket, black waistcoat, bow tie, white wing collar shirt, black evening trousers, black patent shoes

II-1 White shirt, beige trousers, green waistcoat, green ascot, white tap shoes, straw hat

II-2 As 1780 ANCESTOR: white powdered wig, burgundy velvet 18th century coat, cream geometric tapestry waistcoat, olive green breeches, tan tights, black Georgian buckle slippers with red heels
Second entrance as II-1, but no hat and add linen Norfolk jacket with green pocket square

II-4 Red tails, white wing collar shirt, white waistcoat, white bow tie, black evening trousers, black patent shoes, white gloves

II-5 Grey trousers, white wing collar shirt, grey waistcoat, grey morning coat with white carnation, grey gloves, grey cravat with pin, grey top hat, black patent shoes

HERBERT PARCHESTER

I-1   Black jacket, black waistcoat, striped tie, striped black and grey trousers, black shoes and socks, white wing collar shirt, cuff links, watch and chain, spectacles

I-3   As I-1

I-5   Black double breasted dinner jacket, white wing collar shirt, black evening trousers, black bow tie, black shoes

II-1 Light grey jacket with pink rosebud buttonhole, striped tie, white wing collar shirt, striped trousers, black shoes, straw hat with black band

II-2 As II-1 without hat

II-4 Black tails, black evening trousers, white bow tie, white wing collar shirt, white waistcoat, black shoes, white gloves

II-5 Grey morning coat with white carnation, grey waistcoat, grey trousers, grey cravat with pin, black shoes, grey top hat, grey gloves, white wing collar shirt

CHARLES HETHERSETT

I-1   Black morning coat, matching single breasted waistcoat, striped trousers, white wing collar shirt, black boots, black tie, gold cuff links. The above worn throughout except for the following in I-5

ME AND MY GIRL

and II-5: Black tails, black evening trousers, black boots, white wing collar shirt, black bow tie, black waistcoat

LORD BATTERSBY

I-1   Dark blue blazer, white shirt, blue tie with red stripe, grey flannels, brown suede shoes, beige waistcoat

I-5   Black dinner jacket, white wing collar shirt, black evening trousers, black bow tie, black shoes, white gloves

II-1 Blue blazer, white flannels, brown shoes, blue/red striped tie, belt (no braces), straw hat

II-2 1490 ANCESTOR (Henry VII): Black quilted doublet, brown and gold robe with brown velvet cuffs, black tights, black slippers, flat velvet cap with turned up brim
Second entrance: As II-1, no hat

II-4 Black tails, black evening trousers, white wing collar shirt, white waistcoat, white bow tie, black shoes, white gloves

II-5 Grey morning coat with white carnation, grey trousers, grey waistcoat, white wing collar shirt, grey cravat with pin, black shoes, grey top hat, grey gloves

LADY BATTERSBY

I-1   Periwinkle spotted dress with jacket, navy/white shoes, gold and pearl brooch,

	two strand pearl necklace, wedding and engagement rings
I-5	Black Fortuny pleated evening dress with shimmer cape, black shoes with diamond trim, black/gold turban with feathers, diamond earrings, necklace, bracelet, white evening gloves
II-1	Navy/white dress with jacket, navy white shoes, seamed stockings, pearl necklace, pearl stud earrings, diamond brooch, gold bangle and rings as before
II-2	As II-1
II-4	Red/gold strapless evening dress with sequin detail and shawl, gold shoes, gold beaded wreath headdress, pearl rope necklace, off-white evening gloves
II-5	Grey dress and jacket with fur collar, silver shoes, grey hat with organza roses, off-white gloves, diamond brooch

SIR JASPER TRING

I-1	Checked plus fours, white shirt, argyle shirt (green/beige/brown), brown paisley cravat, brown cardigan, suede fronts, ear trumpet, brown suede shoes, yellow knitted waistcoat
I-5	Black velvet jacket, white wing collar shirt, black evening trousers, black bow tie, black patent shoes, black brocade double breasted waistcoat, watch chain

ME AND MY GIRL

II-1 Navy, russett and green stripe blazer, white flannels with belt, brown suede shoes, white shirt, cream cravat, white cotton hat (wicket keeper's type)

II-2 As II-1 without hat

II-4 Red tails, white wing collar shirt, white bow tie, white waistcoat, black evening trousers, black patent shoes, watch chain, white gloves

II-5 Grey morning coat with carnation, grey waistcoat, grey trousers, white wing collar shirt, black patent shoes, grey top hat, grey cravat with pin, grey gloves

CHORUS MEN

N O T E : All trousers are worn with braces (suspenders). COCKNEY trousers have no creases and are hemmed short of a BREAK. All men's trousers are cuffed except black formal trousers.

I-1 GUESTS: All wear windsor collared shirts, four-in-hand ties.
#1) Dark tan three piece suit, brown spectator shoes, hat
#2) Tan two piece suit, rose waistcoat, brown shoes, glasses
#3) Brown plus fours plaid suit, rust waistcoat, burgandy knee socks, brown shoes, plaid woolen grouse
#4) Blue-grey plaid suit, grey waistcoat, grey straw fedora, black and grey spectators, glasses

#5) Camel trousers, blue v-neck sweater, off-white sport coat, blue/white college scarf, tan felt fedora, shoes

#6) Grey trousers, navy double-breasted blazer, straw fedora, brown and tan spectators

CHAUFFEUR: Grey trousers, tan sports coat, hat, brown shoes

CONSTABLE: Dark navy pants, coat, cap, Bobby hat, black boots

3 STOCKBROKERS: Grey pinstripe suit, striped shirts with white wing collar, black striped ties, black leather gloves, black wing tip shoes, black bowler hats, horn rimmed glasses

4 FOOTMEN: white formal shirt, black bow tie, black formal pants, black kid oxfords, green and gold striped waistcoat, green tail coat, white gloves

MAJOR DOMO: As FOOTMEN, but add brass buttons on green tails

MAN IN SUIT OF ARMOR

I-2

CHEF: white chef jacket, apron, hat, blue checked pants, black shoes

MAJOR DOMO: as I-1

3 FOOTMEN: as I-1

4 FOOTMEN: as I-1, but coatless

GARDENER: Brown trousers, work boots, collarless shirt, pullover sweater vest, garden apron, glasses

BOOTBOY: Work boots, striped trousers, collarless shirt, pullover Fair Isle sweater, (tucked in), braces outside

I-3

5 TENNIS PLAYERS: White trousers, sport sweaters in blue or white, white shirts, white tennis shoes and socks.

ME AND MY GIRL

I-4   PUB LOCALS: 2 in brown loafers, knee socks, plus fours, shirts, kerchiefs, pullovers, jackets, caps; 2 in high rubber boots, wool pants, shirts, sweaters, hats; 1 in raincoat; 1 in wool Norfolk jacket
PIANO PLAYER: Brown pants, brown work boots, shirt, brown cardigan

BARTENDER: Brown wool pants, shirt, bow tie, Fair Isle sweater vest, brown work boots

I-5   GUESTS: Black formal trousers, black patent shoes, white formal shirts, black bow ties. 2 in white dinner jackets, 2 in black dinner jackets, 1 in red military jacket, navy trousers with red stripes, black kid ankle boots

PEARLY KING: Black three piece suit patterned with pearl buttons. Pattern on back spells "Lambeth Pearly King", bow tie, wing collar shirt, black work boots

COCKNEY MEN: Brown pants, collarless shirts, kerchiefs, pearled vests, bowler hats (1 in brown pin striped suit)

3 WAITERS: Formal pants and shirts, white waiter jackets, black shoes and bow ties

FOOTMAN: as in I-1

II-1   2 FOOTMEN: as in I, but no coats, no gloves, tap shoes

MAJOR DOMO: as in I

ATHLETIC GUESTS: #1) Light tan trousers with belt, white shirt, tangerine sweater tied around waist, tan argyle socks, brown tap shoes, straw fedora
#2) Dark tan trousers, striped shirt, light blue V-neck pullover sweater, straw fedora
#3) Tan plaid trousers, striped shirt, yellow sleeveless sweater vest, tan fedora, brown tap shoes

GUESTS: #1) White trousers, striped shirt, blue ascot, blue and tan striped sports coat, blue and white tapped spectators, straw fedora
#2) Two piece linen suit, striped shirt, rose ascot, brown tap shoes, straw fedora
#3) Camel trousers, striped shirt and tie, blue pullover sweater vest, brown oxfords, camel fedora
#4) White trousers, belted, white shirt, blue ascot, dark blue striped sports coat, white suede oxfords
#5) Blue grey trousers, grey waistcoat, striped shirt and tie, linen jacket, straw fedora, glasses
#6) Tan trousers, tan shirt, brown ascot, rose plaid vest, brown oxfords, straw fedora
#7) Light grey trousers, cream shirt, gold ascot, gold waistcoat, brown spectators, straw fedora

II-2   ANCESTORS: All ANCESTOR costumes are distressed to look old and moldy. They were buried in these clothes. Dancers'

shoes are tapped. Six selected costumes appear painted on ANCESTOR portraits
#1, (1100) Twelfth century Normal knight
#2, (1300) Fourteenth century armored knight
#3, (1400) Fifteenth century court pageboy
#4, (1440) Richard III
#5, (1490) Henry VII
#6, (1530) Henry VIII
#7, (1550) Sixteenth century Elizabethan Explorer
#8, (1580) Sixteenth century Spanish sailor
#9, (1630) Seventeenth century French cavalier
#10, (1660) Charles II
#11, (1700) Restoration noble
#12, (1750) Eighteenth century red coat
#13, (1810) Nineteenth century Georgian Judge
#14, (1890) Nineteenth century Victorian banker
#15, (1920) Twentieth century Edwardian gentleman

II-3   CONSTABLE: Dark navy pants, coat, cap, bobby hat, black boots
TELEGRAPH BOY: Blue/grey uniform, leather waist pouch
BOB BARKING: Brown pants, plaid shirt, green sweater, apron, cap, boots
LAMP LIGHTER: Shabby long coat, shabby pants, beat up felt hat, boots
3 LAMBETH TRAMPS: dark and tattered

COCKNEY DANCERS: #1, brown pants, sweater vest
#2, Brown pants, brown cardigan

#3, Green pants, Fair Isle sweater
#4, Green pants, black and tan cardigan
#5, Brown plaid pants, waistcoat
#6, Dark grey pants, waistcoat

II-4   2 LIVERIED FOOTMEN: Patent pumps, white tights, white satin breeches, black velvet coats, powdered wigs, white gloves

6 MEN GUESTS: All men wear black patent oxfords, black formal trousers, white formal shirts, white ties, white pique waistcoats, white gloves. Four are in black tail coats, two are in red tail coats. One is in red military coat with navy trousers as in I-5 with white gloves added

II-5   PHOTOGRAPHER: Charcoal trousers, shirt, tie, black shoes, trench coat, cap
PEARLY KING: as in I-5
BOB BARKING: Full pearled suits and caps
2 COCKNEY MEN: Full pearled suits and caps

CHORUS WOMEN:

Note: All ladies wear seamed stockings except in I-3 and II-1. ALL MAIDS, COCKNEY and LAMBETH WOMEN wear seamed cotton Lisle stockings, garter belts, and white cotton knickers

I-1   GUESTS: #1) Navy plaid two piece, slim skirted suit with navy hat, clutch purse and shoes. White gloves, jewelry
#2) Dusty rose dress and jacket, grey fox fur wrap, tan brimmed hat, shoes, clutch purse, gloves, pearl earrings

#3) Apricot three piece suit, pill box hat, tan shoes, clutch purse, gloves, pearl jewelry

#4) Light blue print dress with solid blue jacket, navy shoes, clutch purse, blue and white wide brimmed hat, white gloves, pearl jewelry

#5) Three piece peach ensemble, three quarter coat trimmed in rooster hackle, brown shoes, peach purse, tan gloves, pearl jewelry

#6) Full length brown traveling coat with silver fox wrap, mauve shoes, purse, gloves, brown straw wide brimmed hat, pearl jewelry

HOUSEKEEPER: Black dress and shoes, wide collar cuffs, short wide apron, cameo brooch

4 MAIDS: Black dresses with white collars and cuffs, white bibbed linen aprons with bows, black shoes, white pleated hats

I-2 3 KITCHEN MAIDS: Blue gingham dresses, white collar, cuffs, aprons and mob caps, black shoes

COOK: White dress, apron, hat, glasses, black heeled oxford shoes; padding for size

LADIES MAID: Black dress and pleated cap, white collar, cuffs, and apron, black walking shoes

HOUSEKEEPER: as I-1

I-3 5 TENNIS PLAYERS: 5 different tennis dresses, pink and blue hair scarves, white tennis shoes and socks

I-4 PUB LOCALS: #1) Green pleated skirt, tan blouse, green sweater, tan tam, walking shoes
#2) Brown plaid coat, tan woolen head scarf, brown walking shoes
#3) Green skirt, green plaid coat, brown knit cap, brown walking shoes

I-5 GUESTS: #1) Silver panee velvet with gold beading, tiara, long pearl earrings, silver shoes
#2) Silver snakeskin sheath gown, gold shoes, rhinestone jewelry, down cape
#3) Gunmetal grey gown with amber beaded train and hat, down cape, grey suede shoes, rhinestone jewelry
#4) Seafoam gown with iridescent sequins and pouf ruffled sleeves, butterfly headdress, pewter shoes, rhinestone jewelry
#5) Black and silver sheath gown, black sequin grape hat, black shoes, jet and rhinestone jewelry
#6) Grey satin gown with cut velvet sleeved capelet, long pearl earrings, pewter shoes

PEARLY QUEEN: Maroon suit fully designed with pearl buttons. Pattern on back spells "Lambeth Pearly Queen". Large pearled and plumed picture hat, black shoes with purple bows, purple lace gloves, raspberry blouse

COCKNEY WOMEN: Large plumed and pearled hats, full skirted dresses (1 orange print, 1 purple print, 1 black print)

with full ruffled petticoats, character shoes, paste jewelry

FORMAL MAID: As before, but add organdy hair bow and heart shaped black and white spotted apron

II-1   2 MAIDS: Green print dresses with white collars and cuffs, pleated hats, petticoats, black tap shoes.

GUESTS: #1) Yellow striped cotton sun dress with solid yellow jacket, yellow straw hat, yellow tap shoes, pearl jewelry
#2) Hot pink floral print halter dress, pink straw hat, pink and beige tap shoes, earrings, bracelets
#3) Tangerine print dress, tangerine straw brimmed hat, two tone tap shoes, pearl necklace, earrings, bangle bracelets
#4) Blue floral print dress, lavender blue brimmed hat, blue tap shoes, jewelry
#5) Yellow polka dot dress, yellow straw hat, yellow tap shoes, pearl earrings
#6) Green print dress, green horsehair hat, white lace gloves, green and white shoes, pearl jewelry
#7) Salmon print dress, salmon horsehair hat, salmon taps, pearl necklace, earrings
#8) Lavender print voile dress, lavender hat, mauve shoes, white gloves pearl jewelry
#9) Blue/green print voile dress, blue and white brimmed hat, dark blue slippers, white gloves, pearl jewelry

II-3   PREGNANT COCKNEY: Dirty brown cotton dress, dark green jacket, flat oxfords, brown print hair kerchief, padding

LAMBETH SHOPPER: Dark grey coat, hat, black walking shoes, pocketbook

LAMBETH GIRL: Bright green flouncy dress, high heeled pumps, brown print velvet jacket, green veiled hat, orange lace gloves

MRS. BROWN: Dark print cotton dress, cotton print apron, hair rollers, kerchief over hair, shabby grey cardigan, plaid bedroom slippers, lisles rolled down

BAG LADY: Dirty dress, apron, jacket, hat boots, falling down lisles, large hip and breast padding

COCKNEY DANCERS: #1) Mauve print dress, burgandy hat, brown shoes
#2) Beige print dress, brown straw hat, wine shoes
#3) Pink blouse, brown skirt, rose cardigan, black shoes, brown felt hat
#4) Lavender blouse, green sweater and skirt, blue hair ribbon, tan shoes
#5) Rose blouse, green plaid skirt, dark green sweater, hair ribbon
#6) Two piece lavender dress, blue felt hat, black shoes

II-4   10 GUESTS: All wear evening gloves, evening slippers, rhinestone or pearl jewelry. Four in long black evening gowns, six in long red evening gowns

II-5   PEARLY QUEEN: as in I-5
          MRS. BROWN: Full length pearled coat, plumed pearled hat
          3 FORMAL MAIDS: as in I-5

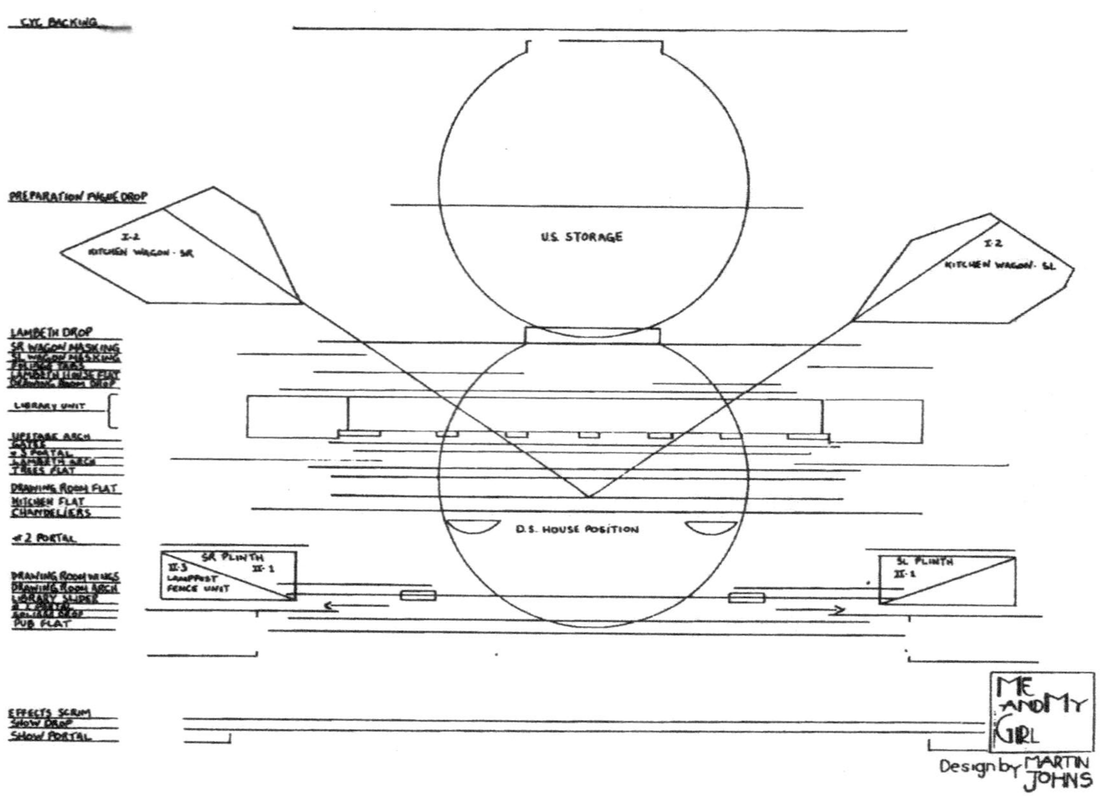
CYC BACKING
PREPARATION PAGE DROP
I-2
KITCHEN WAGON - SR
U.S. STORAGE
I-2
KITCHEN WAGON - SL
LAMBETH DROP
SR WAGON MASKING
SL WAGON MASKING
LIBRARY UNIT
UPSTAGE ARCH
TREES FLAT
DRAWING ROOM FLAT
KITCHEN FLAT
CHANDELIERS
D.S. HOUSE POSITION
#2 PORTAL
SR PLINTH
II-3
II-1
LAMPPOST
FENCE UNIT
SL PLINTH
II-1
DRAWING ROOM WINGS
DRAWING ROOM ARCH
LIBRARY SLIDER
PUB FLAT
EFFECTS SCRIM
SHOW DROP
SHOW PORTAL
ME AND MY GIRL
Design by MARTIN JOHNS